# THE CAPTAIN'S FOLLY

THE SECOND BOOK IN THE CAPTAIN TRILOGY

## Mel J Wallis

Copyright © Mel J Wallis 2022
This book is sold subject to the condition that it shall not, by way of trade or otherwise, be lent, resold, hired out, or otherwise circulated without the publisher's prior consent in any form of binding or cover other than that in which it is published and without a similar condition including this condition being imposed on the subsequent publisher.
The moral right of Mel J Wallis has been asserted.
ISBN-13: 9798363042645

This is a work of fiction. Names, characters, businesses, organizations, places, events and incidents either are the product of the author's imagination or are used fictitiously. Any resemblance to actual persons, living or dead, events, or locales is entirely coincidental.

This book is dedicated to my mum, with whom I first shared the idea of 'The Captain's House' and the ongoing story lines that are continued in the 'The Captain's Folly'. Sadly, she is no longer with us to see my idea come into fruition as a 'real' book. She is missed daily and never more so than when I am writing my Captain trilogy.

# CONTENTS

ACKNOWLEDGEMENTS ..................................................................... *i*
*One* ............................................................................................... *1*
*Two* .............................................................................................. *6*
*Three* .......................................................................................... *10*
*Four* ........................................................................................... *16*
*Five* ............................................................................................ *20*
*Six* .............................................................................................. *25*
*Seven* ......................................................................................... *29*
*Eight* .......................................................................................... *33*
*Nine* ........................................................................................... *37*
*Ten* ............................................................................................. *40*
*Eleven* ........................................................................................ *43*
*Twelve* ....................................................................................... *48*
*Thirteen* ..................................................................................... *52*
*Fourteen* .................................................................................... *58*
*Fifteen* ....................................................................................... *62*
*Sixteen* ...................................................................................... *65*
*Seventeen* .................................................................................. *70*
*Eighteen* .................................................................................... *74*
*Nineteen* .................................................................................... *78*
*Twenty* ...................................................................................... *82*
*Twenty-One* .............................................................................. *85*
*Twenty-Two* .............................................................................. *89*
*Twenty-Three* ............................................................................ *92*
*Twenty-Four* .............................................................................. *96*
*Twenty-Five* .............................................................................. *99*
*Twenty-Six* .............................................................................. *103*
*Twenty-Seven* .......................................................................... *107*
*Twenty-Eight* ........................................................................... *110*
*Twenty-Nine* ............................................................................ *114*
*Thirty* ...................................................................................... *118*
*Thirty-One* .............................................................................. *122*
*Thirty-Two* .............................................................................. *127*
*Thirty-Three* ............................................................................ *131*

| | |
|---|---|
| Thirty-Four | 135 |
| Thirty-Five | 138 |
| Thirty-Six | 141 |
| Thirty-Seven | 145 |
| Thirty-Eight | 149 |
| Thirty-Nine | 154 |
| Forty | 157 |
| Forty-One | 160 |
| Forty-Two | 163 |
| Forty-Three | 167 |
| Forty-Four | 171 |
| Forty-Five | 175 |
| Forty-Six | 178 |
| Forty-Seven | 181 |
| Forty-Eight | 185 |
| Forty-Nine | 189 |
| Fifty | 193 |
| Fifty-One | 196 |
| Fifty-Two | 200 |
| Fifty-Three | 204 |
| Fifty-Four | 208 |
| Fifty-Five | 211 |
| Fifty-Six | 214 |
| Fifty-Seven | 218 |
| Fifty-Eight | 221 |
| Fifty-Nine | 223 |
| Sixty | 227 |
| Sixty-One | 230 |
| Sixty-Two | 234 |
| Sixty-Three | 237 |
| Sixty-Four | 239 |
| ABOUT THE AUTHOR | 242 |

# ACKNOWLEDGEMENTS

I continue to be amazed and often rendered speechless by the ongoing support and encouragement for my writing by my wonderful family and friends. Being speechless, for those who know me, is extremely rare, as I love to talk and tend to chatter incessantly to anyone within earshot who is willing to listen.

My husband, Andy, and my two teenage girls, Amy and Louise, often take second place to my adventures with my fictitious captains, but they never complain. They know only too well that the housework and dinner are not on my 'to do' list when I am tucked away writing or pottering in the garden with the next chapter whirling away in my head.

I know that I am so very lucky to have such a wonderful and supportive family.

My beautiful Spaniel, Lucy, deserves a mention primarily for being my 'furry ears' as my working hearing dog, but also for being my faithful companion at my side on our daily walks together while I plot the next chapter. Sitting patiently at my feet while I scribble some notes, take photos of the countryside that inspires me, or as I watch crows and magpies with an intent fascination when all she really wants is to run, explore, and have her own little 'adventures' without me.

This book would still be in my head without the unwavering support and encouragement of my two close friends, Anne and Sarah, who proofread my finished drafts, help me with editing, and keep me focused.

Finally, I simply must acknowledge all the readers of 'The Captain's House' that have left reviews and sought me out to tell me in person that they enjoyed reading my very first novel. I really must stop doing the 'happy dance' around my living room. It is so unprofessional!

# *One*

It was Christmas Eve and starting to get dark.

The wind was growing in intensity and the light was beginning to fade. The colours of the countryside were turning from a faint, orange hue to a dull, murky grey. As the light faded the warmth of the Christmas season faded too. The wind turned cold and wintry, and the robin fell silent as the night fell.

On the marshes, a short walk away from the village, the nocturnal animals started to stir as the daytime creatures began to sleep. The recent hikers had left, leaving just their footprints in the wet clay. The Kent countryside disappeared along with the distant shoreline in the inky blackness of the night.

The clouds scurried across the sky, chased by the strengthening wind. Then the sky cleared and the moon appeared, bathing the marsh in its milky glow. The bare branches of the trees danced in the moonlight, casting shadows on the well-worn paths which had been carved into the landscape by centuries of Kentish folk.

The individual blades of grass cast miniature shadows of their own, until the shadows faded, and two figures appeared in the moonlight walking along the narrow trackway. In the distance, on the far side of the marsh, smaller figures darted about on the grass. Then, silhouetted in the moonlight just visible in the distance, several more figures appeared.

The outline of their clothes were partly visible, subtly revealing in which century they had lived, loved, and worked. They moved silently in the moonlight. The smaller figures dashing about were children playing tag and the couple slowly walking along the trackway were elderly and stooped over, holding a stick in one hand and their companions' hand in the other.

When the couple got to a small gaggle of trees and bushes, the remains of a long-forgotten folly could be seen, where once atop of the high tower you could have surveyed the coast and countryside for miles around. They stopped and sat on a bench, which was hidden in the shadow of the overhanging branches of several trees which were largely shielding the folly from view. Side by side they sat holding hands, watching the children playing and figures in the distance walking to the seashore laden with heavy backpacks with a solitary dog at their feet. A shrill whistle could be heard faintly in the distance and another dog could be seen sending sheep scurrying in the direction of its master's command.

Then the noises of the children playing grew louder and the quiet conversation of the couple could be heard above the wind. The moonlight intensified as the noise increased. It was as if daylight had returned in the middle of the winter's night. The marsh now belonged to a different time and the people that were once present had reclaimed what was theirs, unbeknown to those sleeping in the nearby village.

The night passed as day for the figures on the marsh, the old couple enjoying a rest on the bench pressed together for warmth and comfort. Their faces alight with delight at their surroundings and their eyes bright with love for each other. Enjoying their time once more as the night slipped past.

Eventually the couple started to fade, and one by one all the figures flickered in the moonlight, visible for only a few moments more as the darkness and the silence regained equilibrium. The children vanished as quickly as they had appeared until just the outline of the marshes fading into the distance could be seen.

The moonlight grew fainter as the light from the dawn grew stronger. The wind dropped and the trees became still. The hedgerow started to bustle as the animals within woke to the light of a new day, Christmas Day.

As the day broke and the still dawn mist hugged the bare wintry marshland, the bleak winter sunlight filtered through the mist onto the hard, frozen land. The frost was thick and glistened like jewels in the light of the sun. Footprints had been left behind, belaying the events of the night-time and the nocturnal visitors from the past. Footprints that should not have been there.

These footprints were discovered by Bert, a lively Spaniel, out for his first walk of the day before the Christmas festivities began back at their cottage. His nose followed their trails across the land with Mickey, his master, following the centuries-old path. While Mickey sat to catch his breath and watch the mist disperse in the morning sun, Bert continued to sniff at the smaller footprints scattered across the surrounding scrub and marsh land. Mickey watched his dog scamper across the marshy field with obvious delight and an odd interest in the frozen grass, until he too spotted the indentation of the footprints that had been left behind and watched as Bert followed what remained of them trodden in deep in the thick layer of frost.

He looked down at the worn path beneath his feet under the bench and noted that they had stopped right there where he was sitting. When he looked behind him, he could see that the frost hadn't formed properly on the back of the bench and there was an outline of what looked remarkably like the backs of two adults sitting close together.

It was very early, and they were usually the first ones on the marsh in the mornings, just him and his dog. It was only just getting light. They had left the cottage in pitch black, knowing their way from familiarity, having lived in the village all their lives. Both he and the spaniel were born there, as were generations before them. He was unsettled and unnerved as he looked around him once more. His spaniel jumped up beside him, sniffed the worn wood of the bench, snuffled quietly, and curled up next to him. Totally at ease and content with his surroundings. The spaniel calmly looked up at his master and rested his head on his trouser leg. All the energy and excitement had left him, and he was content to lay at his master's side, reassuring him that all was well.

Mickey loved to sit on this bench and survey the landscape with the sea on the horizon, barely visible as the sun rose higher in the sky and the night retreated once more. There was always a silence and hush in this place, regardless of the time of day or night. It was his special place, away from the demands of modern life and the bustle of the village. Mickey was a regular at the local pub, The Ship, and propped up the bar for most of the late afternoon into the evening. Bert dictated the pace of his master's life, making him rise early and not linger too long in the pub in the evening when Bert needed another walk. The pair of them walked the same track from the village, past the Captain's House and beyond to this bench twice daily. The wooden slats were worn and the iron frame rusty from the weather and the constant salty assault from the nearby sea. A strange pattern was crudely scratched on the seat of the bench and Mickey often traced the outline of this pattern with his fingers while coming up with fanciful ideas of what it could mean.

Mickey and Bert did not settle down for long as even though he was wrapped up warm and they were huddled together, it was Christmas Day, and he was due back in the village to celebrate the day with his friends. The Ship had closed and had been up for sale for a few months, so Mickey's routine was different, along with the rest of the pub's regulars. Mickey and Bert were off to spend the afternoon with Rose, Tom, and Mowzer in the Captain's House. After a short while Mickey followed Bert back along the track, now noticing the frozen footprints that he hadn't seen on the way there.

He felt the package in this coat pocket and grinned broadly. He had the perfect gift for the new owner of the Captain's House, and he couldn't wait to give the package to Rose. As he touched the package, the wind picked up and he heard a bell ringing in the far distance. *Ting, Ting* ... then a short pause. *Ting, Ting, Ting* ... a longer pause. *Ting*. As he took his fingers off the package it stopped. The wind died down instantly.

Shaking his head, Mickey, with Bert at his side, set off for home.

# *Two*

In the Captain's House, Rose and Tom were stirring as Mowzer, their black-and-white cat, had just awoken them from their slumber with a swipe of his paw at their faces, wanting his breakfast. They had got the house ready for their guests on Christmas Eve, cooked the Christmas turkey a day early, and were planning a lazy day before greeting their friends and family on Boxing Day for their first Christmas in the house, until Rose had impulsively changed their plans at the last-minute the night before at the Christmas Eve Party, inviting Mickey and Bert over on Christmas Day as well.

Rose had met Tom in the summer, and they had grown close, but Tom still hadn't moved into the house with Rose. As her last boyfriend, Mike, had been a slimy character, she needed time before she took the next step of letting Tom move into the house with her on a permanent basis. Tom practically lived there anyway but rented the apartment above his brother's restaurant, never staying more than a couple of nights in a row, sensing Rose's need to go at her speed and have her own space. Rose loved and trusted Tom. They both loved the house and surrounding land, with all its quirkiness, and respected the generations of captains that the house was named after and the Captain's legacies that remained within its walls.

Mowzer bounded down the stairs, taking a big wide detour around the holly swag that adorned the bannisters and the newel post at the bottom of the stairs. He slithered to a stop and came to an ungainly halt in front of a large pile of wrapped Christmas presents by the front door. The cat turned to glare at Rose who was following him down the stairs, she reached down and scooped him up into her arms with a giggle. Mowzer continued to meow his annoyance at her from across her shoulder and then maintained a series of chirrup noises directly into her ear. Rose had put the presents by the front door last night when Mowzer was fast asleep, bringing them down from their many hiding places upstairs, intending to put them under the Christmas tree last night but had retreated upstairs when Tom started to get suspicious. The presents had only got as far as the bottom of the stairs and the front door. Mowzer was stating his indifference to the lack of space and expressing his immediate need for his breakfast.

Mowzer only fell silent when he started to eat his breakfast, a fancy fishy affair that Tom brought with him. Tom's brother, Joe, had cooked it up for him especially using the leftovers from his restaurant. Joe was spending Christmas with his new girlfriend, Tilly, but Tom wanted Mowzer to have a special breakfast so had picked it up on his way over. Having put the kettle on to boil for a morning cuppa, Rose sneaked past Mowzer, who was now completely oblivious to her, and collected the presents from the front door, moving them under the Christmas tree which was taking up most of the space in the little back room. The tree was squeezed in front of the window, with all its Christmas lights twinkling in what remained of the darkness and the dull glow of the morning light. She had to make several journeys from the front door to the tree but eventually all the gifts for their family and friends were under the tree and the house was ready for Christmas.

Rose could not stop herself from fiddling with the decorations on the tree. She had found a box of Christmas decorations in one of the outhouses a few weeks before. Small silver ornaments. Several of flowers, a few birds, holly and myrtle sprigs, anchors, knots, all manner of boats and ships, and an assortment of bells. Beautiful antique ornaments that may not have belonged on the tree or even have been for Christmas. She couldn't resist showing them off on her first Christmas tree in her new home and had tied them on carefully with green cotton. She was disappointed to find that there was no rose in the selection, as over the last year everything seemed to be centred around roses and captains!

*Ting, Ting … Ting, Ting, Ting …*

The ringing was faint at first and it seemed that only Mowzer could hear the sound as he padded into the room to see what she was doing and where the sound was coming from. The fur around his nose and mouth was still encrusted with the remains of his breakfast, fish scales and flesh clinging onto his fur and dripping onto the floorboards as he walked.

*Ting, Ting …*

As Mowzer jumped onto the window seat, brushing against the tree to locate the sound, Rose grabbed a branch of the Christmas tree to stop it toppling over. The tree swayed slightly and all the bells on the tree chimed alongside the bell outside. The same in pitch and frequency, with exactly the same pauses. Now the tree was still but the chiming persisted. The old sounds lingering.

Tom rushed into the room, "I am sure I turned the ringer on your new phone off before I wrapped it!" He pushed a badly wrapped present into her hands with a barely suffused snigger. Rose placed the box next to her ear and replied, "Thank you for ruining the surprise for me, but there is no noise coming from this." Tom snatched the box back and held it up to his ear and shook his head, a puzzled frown on his face. He reached across and opened the window, letting in a blast of cold air with the sound of the bells, now decreasing in volume with every peal. Slowly it tailed off into silence. "That's not church bells, or anything I recognise from around here." Rose shook her head decisively at Tom as she wanted to wait a while before opening any presents to make the festivities last. With a final shake of her head and a wry smile, she backed away from Tom into the kitchen to continue making their morning brew and breakfast.

Tom watched Mowzer clamber down onto the grass beneath the open window and bent down to retrieve the small silver bell that had dropped onto the grass beside him as the cat jumped. His hand searched in the cold frosted grass for the bell. He couldn't find it, but his fingers found something else. Something cold and metallic, which rattled as he lifted it over the sill into the house. It was an old iron ring with three keys of different sizes hanging on it. The keys were so icy that he quickly dropped them onto the window seat cushion and then stretched out again across the sill, fingers splayed to find the bell. He was defeated by the coldness of the air and incessant misty dampness that always seemed to pervade that window near the flowing river that ran alongside the house. He sunk back onto the seat and reached out to take the steaming hot cup of tea that Rose was offering and handed the keys to her. He knew that Rose would be ecstatic about his find but less so about his practical Christmas gift. Typical woman, he thought to himself.

It was Christmas after all, so he didn't share that sentiment with Rose.

## Three

Rose and Tom enjoyed a quiet Christmas dinner, just the two of them as they had planned. The year had been so hectic. They had enjoyed the fantastic Christmas Eve Party the night before at their neighbours, Val and David's home and Bed and Breakfast place, The Lanterns. The village used to gather at the local pub, The Ship, for the annual village Christmas Eve Party but the pub was currently shut due to the financial difficulties of the previous publicans, Bob and Doreen. Joe, Tom's brother, had welcomed the villagers to his bar and restaurant instead, but everyone was missing the focal point and social hub in the actual village. Tom had shut down his restaurant for the Christmas and New Year period on the insistence of his pushy new girlfriend, Tilly, who announced that she needed to spend special 'one on one' time with him over the festive period. Rose secretly thought this was why Tom had suggested a quiet romantic Christmas dinner, but he maintained that it was because they too would need some 'quiet' time after the Christmas Party the night before.

The party at The Lanterns was amazing. Val and David had decorated the house and gardens with tasteful but very expensive Christmas lights and decorations. Val had spent days in the kitchen cooking up a storm and David had bought most of The Ship's surplus stock when they closed in preparation for the party. The local band had serenaded the guests into the early hours of Christmas morning, as everyone was too old to be in bed for Father Christmas's visit. Doreen and Bob had been invited to the party and everyone was expecting them. To everyone's surprise, they did not show up. This meant that everyone had something to gossip about and speculation was rife. The stories people had been coming up with verged from the ridiculous to the amazing. Rose just hoped they were OK and planned to send a text to Doreen to make sure in the coming days. Tom had always said that Rose tended to look after all the 'lame ducks'. He was particularly disgruntled to discover that Rose had invited Mickey and Bert to the house for the late afternoon and into the evening. She had felt sorry for him when Mickey told her that he was spending Christmas day alone and invited him over to share all the 'leftovers' that Tom had pilfered from Val when the party ended the night before.

   Tom had carefully hidden the best bits of his stash from The Lanterns in the back of the pantry and the fridge so that Rose would not offer any to Mickey. Or offer any of the meat savouries to Bert, as she was likely to do. He had carefully placed Mowzer's supper right at the front of the fridge, so Rose didn't have to hunt around for it as Mowzer was due some more fishy restaurant fare for his supper. Rose had plugged her new phone into a wall plug in the kitchen to charge so that she could send her friends and contacts her new number. She was keen to make sure that Mike, her slimy ex, would never contact her again, as he was prone to calling if he was drunk or wanted something. A new phone was sorely needed as Rose used an old model with limited memory space which was rapidly filling up with all the new friends she had made in the village since she moved into the house last year. It was hard to believe that within a year the old, dilapidated 'Captain's House', as it was known locally, was now a cosy home. It still needed more tender loving care in places and the outbuildings were definitely a work in progress. The locals still believed that the house was haunted by the Captain and although the house was now occupied, the ghost of the Captain was still seen regularly through the windows and in the garden. Rose was more than happy to share her home with her ghostly captain. He was there before her and after the events of the last year she firmly believed that the Captain was looking after her and would be there long after her too.

Tom was dozing in the armchair with Mowzer asleep on his lap when Mickey knocked at the front door.

Mickey's knock made Rose jump even though she was expecting it. Hardly anyone knocked at the front door anymore unless they were delivering something. Mickey usually knocked and came in through the back, as did most of her friends and neighbours. The garden at the front was looking neater and more tamed, but the back of the house and her dishevelled outbuildings that were set around a courtyard were more interesting and she was sure her friends were making excuses to have a nose about. They all knew that Rose had ideas for the buildings, but she had kept her cards close to her chest and no one was any the wiser. Even Tom was kept in the dark. Rose had not returned to work in London and had plans for another income stream from her inheritance. She only had a small amount of the £250,00 that came with the house, plot, and outbuildings left. With all the renovations on the main house last year, there was not enough to live on for much longer.

Rose opened the front door, ignoring Mickey as she knelt down to greet Bert first. The spaniel's coat was wet, and his nose had a trace of mud on it. This made no difference to Rose who embraced Bert first with a big cuddle and then went on to give Mickey a welcoming hug too. Rose walked into the kitchen and reached for Mowzer's drying towel off the rail of the oven door and gave Bert a gentle rub to get him warm and dry.

"Ooh, do I get a turn of that too," Mickey laughed and winked at Rose. "It is Christmas after all." Rose giggled and gave him a friendly shove.

"Don't push your luck, cheeky. What would Tom say!" Mickey grinned, his smile reaching from ear to ear across his grizzled, lined face. He had no family left and Rose had offered him companionship at Christmas. He loved her dearly, ever since she had beckoned him over when she spotted him on the footpath eying up her lunch that she was eating in the garden from a distance. They had often shared a lunch together since then. It gave Rose an excuse not to think about the future and find out more about the past from Mickey. For Mickey, it split his day up and gave him someone to talk to. Although the sunny lunches in the garden were just a memory now in the depths of winter, Rose still waved and beckoned him over at least twice a week and they ate their lunch together in front of the fire instead of outside in the sunshine. The sunny lunches of sandwiches and cake had turned into homemade soup and warm crusty bread. Always cake though, no matter what the season. Bert and Mowzer had now reached a truce, but Mowzer did not give up an inch of the house or garden. If he was comfortable, poor old Bert had to walk around him and settle elsewhere regardless.

Mickey reached into his pocket and waved his neatly wrapped Christmas present under Rose's nose and with his other hand he placed a bottle of whisky on the kitchen counter for Tom. Mickey used to collect whisky and had saved the best for a rainy day. He rarely drank at home, preferring to drink in the company of others. He had chosen his finest for Tom just before he had left his cottage that afternoon as he had picked up on a whiff of Tom's dismay when Rose had invited him over on Christmas Day the evening before. He had been determined not to mention that he was alone at Christmas to Rose and had done well until he had let his guard down as the party came to a close. She had wheedled the information out of him then.

Rose was not expecting a Christmas present from Mickey, not one as neatly wrapped with a small red bow atop. She took the parcel with a delighted chuckle and led the way into the back room, putting her fingers to her lips first. She opened the door just ajar so they could all peer around the edge at Tom and Mowzer sleeping beside the Christmas tree. The lights of the tree and the glow of the fire were the only light in the room amid the fading glow of the day from the window. All was at peace.

Until Mowzer's nose twitched, and one eye opened slowly, looking directly at everyone looking around the door. Bert pushed the door wider with his nose and looked in. Mowzer's claws sunk into Tom's upper thigh and the peace was shattered with an immediate howl from Tom as he registered the pain and got a rude awakening. Rose flew across the room to pick Mowzer up before Tom could work out what was happening and throw Mowzer up in the air. After all the commotion, Tom sat bolt upright and looked around him, blinking in the half light. Seeing his guest had arrived he held his breath and counted to three and got up to greet Mickey, noticing straight away that only Rose had a gift in her hand. Mickey followed his eyes and pointed at the kitchen, "I have left something nice for you out there. Fetch a couple of glasses and bring it in. I brought the Christmas 'spirit' with me."

After switching on the lamps, Rose sat down in the other armchair to open her present and Mickey sat alongside her in the accompanying armchair. Bert settled in front of the fire, keeping a close eye on Mowzer who was now perched on the arm of the armchair. Rose opened her present carefully, peeling off the Sellotape slowly so she did not damage the pretty Christmas wrapping paper that was unusually printed with a Christmas Rose design. Mickey saw her looking at the paper, "A local lady printed the wrapping paper, that's her design. It is so pretty and a rose, so I bought some for your present. She uses her designs for other things too. Fabric for cushions, curtains and the like. Isn't she clever?"

"Very talented, how local is she?"

"She lives on the other side of the village and used to work in the city. She didn't like the pace of things in the city so is trying to make her hobby into her business instead. I think she will do very well once she gets known and finds somewhere to work from. Her house is getting taken over with her design work. She has not got room to swing a cat!"

"Interesting," Rose replied, only half listening now as she was trying to prise the lid of the box. It was tight fitting and she needed to use her fingertips to ease the lid away from the base. She lifted the lid very slowly to reveal the treasure within.

# *Four*

It truly was a box of treasures as tightly packed in the box displayed on a scrap of green velvet were ten silver roses with a thin silver chain connecting them all. The roses had stones sparkling around the edges of the petals and were absolutely stunning. Rose lifted the chain of roses from the box and searched for the clasp, thinking that it was a necklace. There were a couple of links missing at both ends but no clasp or sign of one.

"This is too good for me, Mickey, and looks extremely expensive. Are you sure you want to give it to me?"

"I am quite sure, Rose. It was destined for you I reckon. I found it up at the Captain's folly a few weeks ago now, hidden in the undergrowth next to the bench. Well, Bert, did with his nose! I took it home and cleaned it up as I didn't have a clue what it was. It has been there for years I reckon. Bert was digging for Australia that morning. He got down a fair way considering how hard the earth is this time of year with the frost and what not. The land up there is yours, my dear, so anything found up there belongs to you. I will take the credit for finding it though," he retorted with a cheeky wink at Rose and taking a glass of whisky from Tom who had returned to the room just in time to see the gift free from its festive wrappings and hear the end of the conversation.

Rose passed the silver strand of roses to Tom for him to look at. Tom stared in disbelief at the quality of the silver and wondered aloud what the sparkling stone was.

"This trumps my gift of an expensive mobile phone with all the bells and whistles, you know, Mickey, but as this whisky is sublime, I forgive you." Sinking into the small sofa that lined the opposite wall, he put his feet up on the arm of the adjoining armchair. "Speaking of bells, have you heard the unusual bells ringing today, Mickey?"

Mickey pondered the question for a while and sighed, "Yes, I heard bells up at the folly this morning. I thought it was wishful thinking, the tinkling of bells on Christmas morning. I believed it might have been my darling wife wishing me a 'Merry Christmas'. She used to ring the bells in the church you know. I miss her so much; you would have loved her, Rose. I miss Iris so, so much. Mind you, I might have given the roses to her for Christmas instead of you, if she was here."

"We heard bells this morning too, but we were not up as early as you are when you walk Bert up to the folly in the mornings. Did you just call it the Captain's folly?"

"I thought you would have known that it was another one of the Captain's haunts, so to speak. He is often spotted up there on a winter's night, mind. Never in the summer months. I have never seen him myself, but sometimes I have caught the 'look' of a complete building with the tower finished out of the corner of my eye when I am up that way. The ruin still has an intact stairway inside within the main internal walls and you used to be able to look out over the marshes to the sea from the top of the tower. I reckon your old captain used it as a watch tower. Perhaps his wife used it to look out for his return from his long voyages away. Have you ever been to visit your folly, Rose?"

"I have been so busy with all the stuff in the house and the buildings in the courtyard right here, I never thought to traipse up to the folly again. Mum and I walked the boundaries of the property last year when I inherited the house and land. Never felt the urge to explore further until right now. If it weren't dark, I would be up there like a shot. I suppose we could all go up there right now with some torches, what do you reckon, guys?"

Mickey looked at Tom and Tom looked at Mickey and they were in total agreement without a word being said by either of them. Both of them, ensconced in the comfortable easy chairs with a glass of good whiskey in their hands, in front of a glowing log fire. They shook their heads in unison at Rose. Bert lifted his head and watched as Rose raced out of the door and came back with her coat in her hands and a couple of torches. Bert looked at Mickey and then back at Rose and then rested his head back on his front paws and continued to lay prone in front of the fire. Rose reached down and fondled one of Bert's silky spaniel ears and ran her hand down his furry back. The only movement from Bert was a very, very slight wag of his tail. He wasn't going anywhere either.

Rose threw her coat at Tom in frustration, "I will have to wait until tomorrow then, won't I?"

"We have a house full tomorrow, Rose love," Tom replied. "Maybe in a couple of days. You will have to be patient. The folly has waited this long, I am sure it will wait a bit longer."

Rose took the silver strand of roses from Tom and reached across to the Christmas tree, reaching right up to the top branches of the tree. She wound the silver strand around and through the branches. The silver roses next to the Christmas lights glowed and twinkled on the tree. It looked perfect, as if they were meant to be exactly where they were.

"You have found and brought to me my Christmas present from the Captain, you clever man, Mickey! Let's raise a glass for the Captain, guys. Did you forget my glass and whisky, Tom?"

Tom raised his eyes heavenwards and traipsed to the kitchen to get Rose a glass for the toast and grabbed the now charged phone from the kitchen worktop, switching the phone on as he came back with her drink. The phone started to ring as he came into the room. She had given Lisa, her best friend, her new number from the sticker on the side of the box in her last text from her old phone. Rose recognised the number but sat frozen looking at the phone in horror. The phone was making a 'Ting' sound, with the same amount of pauses in between as the bells they had all heard earlier. The 'Ting' sound was identical. It continued for a while and then stopped when Lisa rang off.

"What the hell?" Tom cried as he grabbed the phone. He searched the phone for the ringtones and scrolled through furiously and then sat still and aghast, holding the phone away from him towards Rose. "This ringtone is a recording. I must have recorded it last night, as the time it was recorded is the same time I was wrapping your present after giving it a quick initial charge. I had no clue and never heard those bells last night or intentionally made that recording. How peculiar is that!"

# *Five*

Rose's first Christmas and New Year in her new home flew past in a flurry of festivities. She had a wonderful time with all her family and friends and really started to feel like she belonged in the village as well as in her beloved Captain's House. Tom had only just left that morning to go back to his flat over his brother Joe's restaurant. They had been together since Christmas Eve and Rose was enjoying the peace and quiet of having the house back and being by herself again. The house, although small, had accommodated everyone, but it was a relief to have the Christmas tree outside in the courtyard once more, in its decorative pot and not taking up all the space in the tiny living room at the back of the house. Rose could now see outside from the window without having to push past the Christmas tree's bushy branches. She had missed seeing Mickey when he walked Bert and loved remembering when she had first glimpsed her mysterious stranger, not being sure whether he was real or not. Now she had her view and window seat back, she could sit and gaze across the river into the distance and daydream while she pondered her future and contemplated her past and her connections to the house and its infamous captains.

She desperately needed time to contemplate her future and was so pleased she was finally on her own to think about things. It had been a common theme of many of her conversations over the last few weeks and the Christmas and New Year period. What remained of her inheritance from her Great Aunt was greatly depleted now and she did not have enough to live on for much longer. The house was almost finished and the pot of money that went with the house was almost empty. Rose reckoned she had six months to a year maximum before it ran out completely. She contemplated investing what was left and getting a job locally which would make her instantly financially secure but liked the idea of doing something different and being her own boss. She had lots of ideas but just needed to make a decision and get on with whatever option she decided to go for. The last time she was this indecisive was when she was unsure about keeping the house to live in or whether to sell it on instead. She had got that 'cosy' feeling when she explored the once dilapidated house for the first time. The house was a true 'wreck of the Hesperus' when she first saw it, she thought as she remembered that fateful day. When she had renovated the property the previous year, she had uncovered masses of nautical paraphernalia and the general clutter from the generations of captains that had lived in the house before her.

She collected the holly, pine, and ivy strands that she had wound around the wooden bannisters down the stairs and along the landing to make the house look festive and dropped them into a box at her feet. The house was silent, the radio that Tom always put on when he got up had been switched off by Rose when he left earlier. A kaleidoscope of colours dotted the wooden floor, and her thick black woolly jumper was covered in a rainbow of colours as the faint glow from the winter sun came through the stained-glass window that depicted a galleon on the ocean.

The scent of Christmas from the foliage in her arms dissipated and the fresh briny smell of the sea floated on the air. She continued to look at the window, where the ship seemed to be moving, the colours growing stronger and the wind fresher. The cold air swirled around her feet. The foliage that she had untied and was just balanced and draped around the wooden surfaces came loose and seemed to dance around her feet and body with the wind. Then she lost the bundle of branches that were in her arms into the wind as it increased in strength and felt the motion of the galleon under her feet as it ploughed its way through the choppy seas. Her hand gripped the landing banister, her fingers catching on some splintering underneath as she held on tight to keep her balance. As she started to panic and took a deep breath to steady herself, there was a gentle pressure on her shoulders. A kind presence alongside her and faint whisper in her ear. She was reassured and comforted all at once. As she steadied her breath, the wind died down around her and the ship was still once more in the confines of the leaded pattern in the glass of the windowpane.

The stairs and landing were covered in branches, the box had fallen to the bottom of the stairs by the front door and a bemused Mowzer was peering up at her, blinking in the sunlight, clearly just awoken from his daily slumber. He gingerly tiptoed across the debris to Rose and jumped into her arms to look over her shoulder, head tilted to one side ready to rub his chin into his friend, but by the time he had got there, the presence was gone, and it was just Mowzer and Rose.

It took Rose ages to gather up the decorations that were strewn everywhere with Mowzer offering her his 'kind of' help, playing with any swag she picked up, hiding and jumping out at her in the bigger piles. She picked up the last of it and looked around for any stray bits that might be in any obscure places and saw a single stem stuck in the splintered wood that she had caught her fingers on earlier. When she looked underneath the bannisters, she saw a small carving in the polished patina of the wood which was the cause of the splintering. It looked for all intents and purposes like a roughly hewn arrow pointing over the stairs to the window. Exactly parallel to the bottom of the stained-glass window. How odd!

She lobbed a single stem of ivy over the handrail and onto the stairs below for Mowzer to continue their game, but he was nowhere to be seen. Disappointed, she traipsed down the stairs and picked up the full box of foliage ready to take outside and throw into the compost bin that Tom had created for her in the corner of the garden. It seemed remarkably heavy and, as she lifted the corner of the box, a little black-and-white furry head popped up from beneath the greenery. Mowzer purred and looked very smug. He probably thought he had won the game, until she gave him a little shove to unceremoniously turf him out of the box on the way to the back door, without spilling the contents over the floor.

As she opened the back door, a cold wind blew in, so she grabbed her coat from a hook just inside the door, wedged her feet into her welly boots that were waiting for her on the back door mat, and stuffed her arms into her coat. Before she picked up the box once more, she pulled up her hood over her head and, with her head lowered into the wind, she stepped out into the garden with the box once again in her hands. Within seconds her hood was blown off her head and her hair was blown into disarray by the wind. It took mere minutes to race to the compost heap and back indoors and, in that time, she was chilled right through. Mowzer had not followed her out, he was curled up on the kitchen windowsill and was snoring softly when she returned.

She spotted Mowzer dozing, after removing her coat and running her fingers through her hair, on the windowsill and crossed the kitchen to stand and stroke his fur. She could see the folly in the far distance, a shadowy presence that she had still not managed to visit. It seemed as if she always had a houseful over Christmas. Something for another day. She still felt the comforting presence of her captain from moments ago, which was helping her make her mind up about the future. She knew precisely what she wanted to do and hopefully how to bring in the money she needed to stay in the house and make a living. It didn't involve another job, another office, or travel. Rose had just what she wanted right there. Her house and inheritance.

## Six

It was late afternoon before she had the chance to sit down and look at the notes she had made about her future the year before. Back then she had listed the pros and cons to every business idea, every personal ambition, and every 'pie in the sky' dream. In the bedroom, she curled up in the armchair that she had inherited along with her home. It was well worn; she could sink into the seat and rest her head on the back of the chair. It was one of her favourite thinking spaces in the house, the other was the window seat overlooking the river at the back of the house. She was all too easily distracted with the view from the back window and the folly in the far distance.

It was getting dark. Mowzer had already had his supper and was snoozing on the arm of the chair beside her. She rested her notes on the opposite arm. She had carefully read through all of her ideas again and again. This wasn't really necessary as she knew most of them by heart. Some of them weren't practical and some were simply ridiculous. She giggled as she read the silly, ludicrous ones again. She blamed the TV programme she had watched before making her list. The presenter had urged everyone to follow their dreams, all of their dreams. At the very least make them seem real by writing them down and giving them proper consideration. She had followed the advice blindly at that time and procrastinated ever since. Rose had not discussed her ideas with anyone and really didn't want to. When she inherited the house, her then boyfriend, Mike, had tried his utmost to get her to sell the property and it had left her with nasty memories. She was shocked that she hadn't seen his jealous nature or sly ways and had just focussed on what an extremely good-looking guy he was while going out with him. She had been sucked into his lies and his idea of what constitutes a 'perfect' girlfriend. She suspected that he had always had more than one girlfriend on the go and she was just one of many dotted around the country.

She had wavered in her relationship with Tom, who she had met and fallen in love with after she had decided to leave Mike, but before she had got the chance to tell him. She broke a cardinal rule of her own by dating two men at the same time, but it was love at first sight when she had met Tom. She was still a little uneasy as Tom seemed too good to be true, but he was strong, honest, and loved the very bones of her. She was very conscious of how lucky she was but still planned on keeping the romance slow for a while. Until her head caught up with her heart at least!

She considered going to stay at her mum and dad's house for the weekend. They would love to have her, but she wanted to make all her decisions in her home. This house was an integral part of her life now and she trusted the decisions that she made there. She was more confident than she ever was before she had moved in. She had made lots of new friends while settling into her new home and in the village and she wanted to work with her inheritance and make it work for her too. She believed that she was given the legacy for a reason surely, not just because she shared a name with her batty great-aunt who left all she owned to her. Val, her closest neighbour, constantly teased her that she was becoming a recluse like the same aunt, who she was told never left the village in her lifetime and rarely left the house or land that surrounded it. Rose wondered if her great-aunt ever ventured as far as the folly. She never seemed to get there either!

Rose sighed with relief when she had re-read her notes from cover to cover several times over, as she came to the same final decision that she had when she had made the notes in the first place. Every time she read them, the little voice in her head informed her that it was risky, and she needed to make sure that it worked. The same voice told her that she lacked the confidence and business acumen to drive her ideas into fruition. This time she listened to the Captain. The voice that had whispered into her ear that morning on the stairs. She knew his voice so well. His voice wasn't quite the same as the last time she had heard it. Or as she remembered from her dreams, but it was familiar. It was a voice she would always trust.

'Follow what you see. You have everything you need right here', the Captain had whispered softly into her ear.

The roughly hewed arrow her fingers had found at the same time she heard the Captain showed her the way, pointing through the stained-glass window to the cluster of outbuildings and the courtyard beyond. This was where her ideas lay. Which ideas should she choose? She had listed them all but already had one in motion, the one she had set her heart on. She had let a portion of one of the outbuildings to Steve, one of her first friends in the village and the guy that had helped her repair her house and make it a home once more. She had leaned on him heavily when she first arrived so much so that he had asked her out on a date, thinking that she liked him as more than a friend too. When he realised that this was not the case, it had caused some acute embarrassment to the pair of them, but that awkwardness was firmly in the past, and they were good friends. Steve stored most of his equipment, tools, and building supplies in this building and was happy to pay to do so. She unintentionally had an additional source of income coming in which was currently paying for her weekly food shop, as he paid cash to her every week. She had typed an invoice/receipt for him for his tax return paperwork using her name as a letterhead, but she had typed **THE CAPTAIN'S HOUSE** in bold, capitals, and underlined. She was so excited to find the sign with 'The Captain's House' painted in flowing script hidden in the hedges surrounding her garden and had taken to using this, as well as number 'one' that was listed as her address. 'One' was the only house in the lane and was used as a default for her house, as the name of her house had been lost in the post office records. However, the locals had always referred to the house as 'The Captain's House' and so did she.

Could she use the 'Captain' as her business name? The calculations were healthy, and she could make enough to live on, letting out the rest of the outbuildings to other businesses while she made her own plans. Who, what, or how were left undecided as Rose drifted off to sleep, her notes fell from her hand as she slept. The murmur was faint, very faint at first and grew louder as she slept. 'Follow what you see. You have everything you need right here', whispered again and again into her ear. Mowzer stirred and jumped down from the arm of the chair, following the dust motes as they rose from the floor in sections, swirling in the air, as if someone were walking across the floor, unseen by all, but Mowzer who devotedly trotted behind his captain once more.

## Seven

Rose slept in the following morning as Mowzer did not wake her as usual with a swipe of the paw when he got hungry and wanted his breakfast. The natural light was coming through the curtains that had replaced the sailcloth she had used as a window covering in the first few weeks. The cream curtains were very girly, covered in large blousy roses. They weren't enough to keep the natural light from creeping into the corners of the room and waking Rose gently as the morning grew lighter. She was still waiting for the original window shutters to be rehung when Steve had worked his magic on them.

Rose had stumbled into bed in the early hours after falling asleep in the armchair the night before. She had finally made her decision on her future, the house, and everything else around it. It was as if now she had put her thoughts in order, she could finally sleep deeply once more. She wasn't consciously aware that she had been worrying about anything, but she was subconsciously aware that she was postponing the inevitable.

As her mind was ordered, so was her sleep, and she slept right through to nearly midday, with no Mowzer around to rouse her. She woke naturally and because this hadn't happened since befriending Mowzer, Rose was in somewhat of a daze. She looked around for her bearings and reached out to her mobile phone to see what the time was. She sat upright and clutched the phone to her chest in surprise when she realised exactly what the time was and looked around her for Mowzer, expecting to find him dozing at her feet, or cheekily reposed alongside her on the adjoining pillow. There was no sign of him so she grabbed her dressing gown from the bottom of the bed and ran downstairs barefoot to look for him. Peeking in every room with no luck, she unlocked the back door and opened it a chink. She then stood back waiting for Mowzer to trot in through the gap, but he didn't. The only thing that came in through the gap was a couple of flakes of snow.

Rose peered around the side of the door, grabbing her dressing gown and pulling it around her tightly before she looked out. There were more than a couple of flakes of snow falling. As she looked up skyward, the sky was full of snow, it was snowing hard and had been for several hours it seemed. There was a couple of inches of snow on the ground already. It was so dark, dismal, and cold outside, even for the middle of the day, Rose went to shut the door, but a noise in the distance made her pause and listen. Was it the faint sound of a bell? The bells hadn't been heard since Christmas Day, unless her phone rang. She hadn't the heart to change the impromptu ringtone. Unlike Tom, she liked the sound of the bells and didn't find it sinister or spooky at all. She listened hard and pulled her dressing gown tighter still to keep the cold out. It wasn't a bell, but it was a jiggling sound that was getting closer. Then there was a short meow and Mowzer came into view, picking his paws up high with his nose higher in distaste at the snow reaching up to the top of his legs as his walk broke into a trot. The jingle was Mowzer's name tag on his collar making a noise as he moved through the snow. He picked up speed as he got closer to the door and slid in, shaking snow from his fur as he drew level with her bare feet. She shut the door after him and watched him drip water across the floor as the snow melted from his fur onto the floorboards. He sat indignantly next to his empty food bowl and proceeded to wash himself while waiting for Rose to get his 'late' breakfast.

Rose did not pander to his wishes straight away. She stood transfixed by the snow falling outside the window, making everything white. She couldn't really see the outbuildings as the snow was getting heavier by the second and the folly had vanished from sight in the distance. Rose was excited to see the snow. She had just replenished her groceries and had a good supply of logs for the fire in the house stacked neatly by the fireplace and in the wood store. She had her emergency candles and other stuff packed ready in two boxes, one for upstairs and one for downstairs that Steve had given her for Christmas. An unusual gift, but as practical as her friend, Steve, always was. Two old wooden wine boxes with fancy labels, but not containing any fancy wine. Much to Tom's dismay, making his grin go sideways when he saw what was in the box after all. Just emergency stuff, as Steve had lived in this part of Kent all his life and knew about the power cuts and extreme weather that could come in from the coast and across the marshes. Rose was not worried at all, she had a stack of books, stash of chocolate and wine given to her for Christmas, and a freezer full of leftovers from the Christmas meals and snacks that hadn't been eaten by Tom before he left. Snow is always lovely, if you are prepared and you don't have to be or go anywhere, Rose thought as she watched the swirls of snow fall out of the sky and settle on the ground. As the snow thickened, the reflection of the snow made the daylight seem brighter and forced her attention back to the present.

So did Mowzer. He didn't care for Rose's inattention and wound his little wet body around her bare legs and tiptoed over her feet. He wanted his breakfast and wouldn't settle until he had some. Rose opened the cupboard where she kept his food and took a food pouch from the open box, mentally assessing if she had enough food to keep Mowzer happy if the bad weather continued for a few days. Seeing she had plenty, she opened the pouch for Mowzer and tipped all of it into his bowl.

When she had eaten her own breakfast, she curled up once more upstairs in the armchair. She had her laptop perched on the arm and was researching her ideas for the outbuildings, stables, and courtyard. She was making excellent progress when the lights flickered and went out. It was barely three o'clock in the afternoon, but it was getting dark fast. She was glad she had eaten a large fried breakfast as she doubted she would have a cooked meal for dinner, it was looking likely she would end up with a sandwich if the power didn't come back on. She had forgotten to plug her laptop in to charge for a few days, so she had minimal power left. She shut the laptop down and reached for her notes and a pen instead. Then she picked the OS map from the floor, folded it into a neat square, and gazed with renewed interest at the whereabouts of the folly on the map. How unusual. How on earth would the folly fit into her plans? What was it there for and what could she do with it?

## *Eight*

The snow continued to fall steadily, the house grew quiet and still as the snow muffled the sounds from outside. Rose was lucky not to be troubled by excessive road noise and only had a few cars drive past on their way to the village or the coast most days. However, as the snow settled, all the noises of the outside world receded and the silence grew. Rose was alone with her thoughts, and she had spent most of the day busy scribbling timelines, listing people to talk to, and income streams into her notebook. She was starting to scribble extra points into the margins as her notebook had no more space to write on. She really needed to transfer the contents onto her laptop, into a spreadsheet, and onto emails, ready to set her plans in motion. Rose loved stationary, loved her notebooks, a new one for every new idea. Her mum had always bought her a new notebook, pencil case and pens at the start of every school year. She had loved her yearly treat, which had encouraged her to spend a small fortune on paper stuff and stationery ever since at the start of a new project, but her dad had to nag her to update the software on her laptop or phone. She was a 'paper' girl at heart.

Her phone had trilled all day with text messages from her mum and dad, Val, Steve, and Tom, all with offers for her to visit and sit out the weather with them, or for them to visit and stay with her. Rose had declined all of them with curt dismissal texts, getting more and more cross that everyone thought she couldn't cope with a bit of snow. She had Mowzer for company and Val was walking distance up the lane if push came to shove. She was happy to be left alone for a few days at least.

Tom continued to bombard her with texts trying to get her to change her mind. He even wanted her to scoop up Mowzer in a cat basket and sit out the snow in his flat. He hadn't offered to stay with her at the house, which was a surprise as she was coming round to the idea of him moving in with her one day. It was ironic really that after thinking that he was moving too fast, he was now not only moving too slow, but he was hesitating to move into the house with her after all. Or was it because it was the winter months, as it was more of an effort to live with her in the winter? There were fireplaces in every room, and she loved to use all of them if she was going to be spending any length of time in a room. She loved the romance of a log fire in the bedroom and making love all cosy and warm in front of the glow. Tom was a pragmatic, sensible man and couldn't see the sense of a fire for a couple of hours then falling asleep and letting it go out so there was no warmth to greet you in the morning. Just piles of wood ash to be swept out and another fire to lay. Another job to be done in the morning. He believed that real fires were great, but it would be just as good if they were electric or gas that you switched on and off as and when you needed the heat. No mess, no getting firewood, chopping the wood, stacking it, keeping it dry, and venturing into the cold to bring it in. Invariably it was him that did most of the 'wood' jobs when he stayed there.

However, Rose started to change her mind, as the snow continued to fall well into the evening, when the power stayed off, and the darkness begun to encroach into the house. Mowzer had sunk into the snow when she had let him out a few hours ago and he had not yet returned so she was on her own in the back room. Warm and cosy in front of the fire.

The silence was undeniably oppressive now. The warm amber glow from the log fire burning bright in the grate was fading, taking the warmth too. Rose had scattered battery-operated lamps and candles throughout the house when she had seen the snow falling but had only switched them on in the rooms she was using; the back room, kitchen, and bedroom. She planned to use them as you would a light switch and switch them on as you go. She prodded the fire with a poker and added another log to increase the size, warmth, and cosy glow. It didn't work – the larger log sat atop the glowing embers and dampened the fire right down. No new sparks caught the new log, despite her prodding and poking, and a plume of grey smoke drifted ominously up the chimney with whiffs of smoke surrounding Rose and making her cough and splutter. She wiped her eyes with her hands as the smoke assailed her, making her eyes water. It made her vision blurry. From kneeling to attend to the fire, she sat down on the back of her heels and threw the poker onto the hearth, with tears of frustration. She felt her temper brewing as her tears welled and fought against both emotions. Barely able to see now through her tears, she looked out into the darkness beyond the house and at the odd flake of snow that could be seen in the gloom. Her eyes caught a glimmer of movement. She was unsure if it was outside or inside the room. The movement was slow, pronounced, and certain. She felt a creepy, unsettling sensation and blinked hard to make the vision clearer, reaching for the poker she had thrown in her temper. She wanted something in her hand, a weapon, something heavy, something that would do damage. Rose didn't want to admit it but she was scared right through, as she didn't know whether it was inside or outside. She scrabbled for the poker and, with it in her hand, she shuffled forward towards the window on her knees. Her hand waved the poker in front of her as her eyes tried to focus once more. The darkness increased as her vision returned. The lamps and candles went out.

In the dark there was movement in her peripheral vision coming from the direction of the window. There was definitely a presence, looking out or looking in, tapping in desperation at the glass.

Where was her captain? Her protector? The ghostly custodian of the house? She wished hard for his comforting presence, his whispers, his words. Nothing. Nothing at all.

## *Nine*

*Ting, Ting ... Ting, Ting, Ting ...*

It was faint, very faint. The bells resonating in the far, far distance. Through the darkness, the ting got louder and more pronounced. The bells changed in frequency, recurring faster and faster and then fading away once again. They ebbed and flowed as Rose listened hard, relishing the familiarity. In the darkness she reached for her phone, hoping it was someone calling her, hoping they would hold on until she answered. The screen would have lit up if someone were calling. There was no light. Nothing to help her find her phone. There was just blackness all around her.

*Ting, Ting ... Ting, Ting, Ting* was answered by a *tap, tap, tap*. Something hard was tapping on the glass. The window was wrenched open, and there it hung, until the darkness receded, the lamps flickered on, and Rose could see once more through her tears.

It seemed as if the bells were in the room with her for a split second and in that moment the oppressive fog lifted, replaced with a joyful glee. The sparks flew from the burnt log instantly, catching the newly placed log and producing hot, flickering flames that danced as the bells faded until she couldn't hear them anymore.

She moved swiftly to find her phone and saw it on the window seat where she had left it earlier after answering Tom's many texts. She grabbed it and with her other hand reached for the clasp and swung the window shut. She checked for any missed calls, and there weren't any listed. She then looked up and out of the window. The windows had their usual layer of condensation on them but there were two handprints visible on the glass. Two handprints and an impression of the tip of a nose. She lifted her hands to the prints and held them over the outline. The outline of the prints were slightly smaller than her hands, but not much, there was a blur on the imprint of the left hand, a slight scratch on the glass from a ring worn on the wedding finger. She stretched her hands to the glass, searching for a connection, any connection as she felt so alone and abandoned. She touched the glass with her fingertips first and then made the connection with her palms on the handprints. Different sizes but now together, her hands fused to the glass. The glass should have been cold, after all it was still snowing, but it was warm, as if someone had physically touched the glass and had just moved away. Rose could not bear to take her hands away and leant forward so her nose pressed against the glass, mirroring the clear smudge that was already there. She stayed that way for some time, soaking up the emotions of the past and trying to understand this new oddity of the house.

Up until then she had been frightened, an entirely new sensation for her in her new home, feeling the way she did about her cherished house. She had been told many stories about her house from her friends and other local people. Several of which had remarked that they never went that way or anywhere near her house after dark. Others were amazed that she was happy to live right there in a haunted house when she could have lived in a similar sized house in the village with close neighbours. The folly had chilling stories of its own and the footpath that Mickey used daily to walk Bert was hardly ever used by other dog walkers in the area. Their dogs wouldn't go near the folly and refused to walk that way, whining and pulling when reaching the fork in the footpath to take another route to the sea.

Mickey and Bert loved the solitude and preferred to walk alone. Indeed, if Mickey spied another person while walking, he turned the other way or hid himself and Bert if he saw them first. Mickey loved to chat but on his terms, especially with a drink in his hands. He had no time for endless pointless gossip.

She closed her eyes to still her mind. She could see a buoy topped with a bell rung by the rocking of the waves, marking the starboard side of the coastal waters aiding her captain's ship returning home. She could see the buoy being tossed up and down in the sea and the sound of the bell ringing again and again in her head. The connection was so strong that she felt the pulse of another woman whose hands she held in hers on the windowpane, through the centuries. The woman who had waited patiently for her captain for many months, fearing him lost at sea. Lost to her forever and whose strength had allowed her to tune in and listen out for the bell buoys several miles out to sea. Hoping that they would foretell his return and lift the depression that was all encompassing for her and the house.

In those moments Rose and she were one, lost in the same moment in different times. United in their love of their captain and his house. Waiting to meet again.

## *Ten*

That connection was all she needed to feel reassured and secure in the house again. She stayed still, sitting by the fire, hugging her knees to her chest after sensing someone's hands in her own through the mists of time. She was alone, with the sense of a female presence all around her, warm and comforting. She felt at peace again, calmed by the knowledge that the Captain was returning home safely once more. She had felt the anguish of their parting, their time apart and the wonderful sense of excitement that he was returning to the house once more.

As she watched the flames dance in the fireplace, consuming the logs with a surprising ferocity, she thought about the Captain, recollecting the recent quiet whispers in her ear and the timely advice he had offered when she had needed it. She had always felt a connection to the house and to him, but there had been something niggling her. His voice sounded different. His tone was more nasally, but more softly spoken, less gruff. If his voice had changed, was it the same captain? As she stood up, she picked up the old captain's hat that had spent the last few weeks on the mantelpiece. It didn't seem to fit her conundrum, so she replaced it once more on the mantelpiece. There was something amiss. Puzzled, she sat down in the armchair and looked hard around the room, her eyes coming to rest again at his hat sitting in its regular place – the mantelpiece.

When she first moved into the house, the Captain's hat seemed to move daily and Mowzer was often found curled up asleep in the hat wherever it ended up. These days the hat resided on the mantelpiece over the fire and resolutely stayed put.

Rose, although comforted and no longer disturbed by the distinct handprints on the window which were slowly fading from view, she didn't want to leave the comfort of the fire. She knew she had to open the back door and call Mowzer in for the night. He loved to wander and, in the summertime, she didn't worry so much about him, but tonight with the snow falling she wanted him safe and sound indoors with her. She tiptoed to the back door, opened it, and peered out into the darkness as she was wont to do. She couldn't see Mowzer, but she could see a black shape coming towards her and getting bigger as it got closer. She screamed and slammed the door, fumbling at the key in the lock and locking it tight against the shape. Within seconds there was a loud hammering on the door and the sound of a male voice trying to make himself heard against the sound of the wind. She leaned on the door with her back and gazed around the kitchen for something to arm herself with for the second time that day. The shouts grew louder and more impatient. Then it was quiet for a moment and the shadow could be seen at the window, hands tapping against the glass with increasing urgency. There was a smaller movement to the side of the shadow looking in with bright, orangey eyes, which glittered as they caught the flickering light from the candle burning in the hurricane lamp on the windowsill. The eyes grew brighter and bigger, and it leapt at the window in a bold big movement. A flash of white caught her eyes in an all-too-familiar shape. She spluttered a sigh of relief, realising that she had been holding her breath in horror for there was absolutely no need. It was Mowzer on her windowsill looking to come in out of the snow. She opened the window a small way for his little body to wind his way indoors, but not letting whatever the big shadow was in as well. Out of the darkness, a hand grabbed the window frame, holding it tight and open, and another set of eyes, piercing blue eyes, met hers.

Rose giggled as she felt very silly. Those eyes were as familiar to her as her own. They belonged to Tom. No one sinister, nothing scary, just her Tom. A typical man, he had ignored her protestations of independence and when she wouldn't come to him, he came to her. It had taken some time for him to walk to the house from the village where he had abandoned his car as the snow had become too deep to drive safely. The lanes were now covered with a thick layer of deep snow which was settling fast.

She let him in and fell into his arms. He enveloped her in a big hug, transferring the cold of the outside from his coat onto her jumper. She didn't care. She didn't pull away, just stood there being hugged, reassured, and loved, all thoughts of independence flung from her mind in that instant. She sighed and heard an answering echo in a different female voice. Her fingertips and palms tingled. That connection again.

The women of the house were linked together, emotions in unison as they welcomed their men home once again.

## *Eleven*

Mowzer crept across the kitchen floor silently while they embraced, ate his dinner quietly, and then dashed upstairs to stake his claim on the bed before Rose and Tom. Tom was far too cold to rush Rose into bed, so Mowzer could have taken his time with his dinner. Mowzer walked a slow circle several times before settling at the end of the bed, then curled up into a tight ball. His fur was still damp from the snow, making the bed wet, so the dampness spread straight into the duvet around him.

Tom took his wet coat, scarf, and gloves off and hung them on a hook by the back door. He couldn't fit all of his wet outer garments on the one hook, so he went to put his hat on the adjoining one but saw that Rose had hung the trio of old keys he had found on Christmas Day there.

"Have you found out what these keys belong to yet, Rose?" he asked, picking them up and replacing his hat on the now empty hook.

"Not yet," she replied, "I have been too busy planning stuff today, trying to take my mind off the snow."

"I bet you have. Why don't you tell me all about your plans over dinner? What were you planning to eat, I can't smell anything cooking? Has the power gone off?"

He flicked the light switch with his fingers, and nothing happened. He then noticed the battery-lit candles lining the windowsill and a larger one on the countertop.

"Crazy question, I can see you haven't got any electricity, or have you another romantic guest, apart from me? Is that why you didn't want me to come?" he said as he ran his fingers through her hair, brushing the side of her cheek with them.

Rose sighed once more and this time the echo was more pronounced and louder. Another female voice sighed with her. Tom stood back with a jolt and stared intently at her for the second time that evening. His blue eyes twinkling with humour which faded into curiosity at the echo to Rose's voice. He leaned towards her again and Rose looked into his eyes and their lips met with a tender kiss which was full of promise and deepened quickly into a fierce passion. The kiss lingered, neither of them wanting to pull away. When they did, Rose took a deep breath. There was another sigh, Tom only heard one sigh, but it wasn't Rose's. He was still holding her shoulders with his hands, still close enough to her mouth to hear even the quietest sigh. She made no noise, but he felt her expel her breath. The audible sigh was an echo in his ear. Baffled, he felt a breath close to his ear and heard a whisper, a female voice, but he couldn't make out the words. A sigh, a whisper, and then a giggle.

The giggle was unmistakably Rose as she leant in for another taste. As they kissed again, the giggles persisted. This time it was not Rose, the giggle although similar was not the same. Tom listened to the giggles as Rose pulled away. She held Tom close and laid her head on his shoulder. The giggles resounded around them and then with a single, lone sigh it was quiet once more.

Mowzer sat up bolt upright on the bed, listening to the giggles coming from the kitchen. He knew that voice and sensed that connections were settling at the house once more. He leapt from the bed onto the chair and continued to scramble under the heap of discarded clean clothes that Rose had left on the chair when she got dressed that morning. At the back of the chair, he found what he was looking for: a scrap of material, old and worn. The edge of the material was hemmed and there were little roses embroidered all around the outside. It was a pretty scrap. Finding what he was looking for, Mowzer settled once more on the clean clothes and then, resting his furry head on his paws, he went back to sleep.

Downstairs, Tom held Rose in his arms and looked at the kitchen over Rose's shoulder. Rose had told him all about her captain and he had felt his presence too, but never a female. He thought that he should be perturbed, defensive, or plain worried about the sighs, giggles, and whispers in his ear. Rose did not seem to have noticed or cared, as she nestled in his arms.

Rose broke away first and pointed at the pantry and at the stairs with each hand. She really didn't care where they went first or what they did. She was hungry for food and Tom but didn't care which order. Happy to let Tom decide. His answer was unpredictable but not entirely unexpected. He wanted a bath, clean clothes and while he was doing that, she could either get into bed or make something to eat. Completely bemused, but secretly pleased, she followed Tom upstairs and they entered the bedroom together. Tom left his phone facing upward on the bed and there was enough light to see around the room.

"Oh my god, Mowzer, you are wet and sitting on my freshly washed, clean clothes, you scoundrel, you!" She scooped him up and dabbed a crumb of fishy paste from his chin with her finger. He always saved some for later on his chin! His legs dangled helplessly in her grasp, and he knew she was cross as she normally cradled him like a baby. The scrap of fabric fell onto the floor as she tossed him gently but unceremoniously on the bed. She put him down in the middle of the bed as she noticed the wet patch from his previous slumbers at the end.

She picked up the scrap of fabric from the floor, recognising the faded green colour and entranced by the pretty row of roses embroidered onto the fabric. So engrossed was she that she failed to see Tom, now naked, walk past her into the bathroom to run his bath.

The power had been off for several hours, so the bathroom was in darkness. Tom fumbled around in the dark and managed to put the plug in the bath and turn on the hot tap. He wandered back into the bedroom past Rose to find something to light up the bathroom while he had a bath. He was still naked. Rose was now perched on the edge of the bed running the cloth through her fingers, she had seen something this shade before but where? The pipes gurgled and squeaked as the water ebbed into the bathtub in its normal sedate fashion. When Tom dipped his toe into the bath to test the temperature it was tepid, just lukewarm. He was grumbling his distaste and lowering himself into the water when she appeared in the doorway.

She came into the dim light from the candle that Tom had just found and placed on the edge of the bath a moment earlier. Tom was dismayed to see her dressed head to toe in a flowery dress. It was very pretty, but it was not what he was expecting her to wear for him in bed! As she came towards him, she held her hands out to show him what she was holding. The flame of the candle caught a draught, flickered, and then went out.

Relighting itself seconds later, it revealed Rose dressed as she was in the kitchen, no flowery dress in sight. She was holding a remnant of the floral dress in her hands which clearly showed the distinct pattern of the cuff, the neckline, and the hem of the dress. The embroidered roses were identical to that of the floral dress he had seen her wearing moments earlier. Blinking furiously in the candlelight, he laid back and sank into the water up to his ears. The sighs, giggles, and whispers followed him under the water. Who was it he had seen before in the half-light then? It wasn't Rose, although she looked exactly like her, she really did. When he opened his eyes as he resurfaced, he was unsure who would be sitting on the edge of the bathtub waiting for him.

It was Rose who was sat on the edge of the bath, getting all inquisitive and sentimental about the fabric in her hands. Tom shooed her out of the bathroom and shut the door, unwilling to share his soak with either Rose or her ghostly companion. The water was tepid, but he stayed in the bath until the water went cold, dozing from time to time. Rose was waiting for him, curled up next to her precious cat, until she fell into a deep sleep like Mowzer, who was overcome by his tiredness after traipsing through the snow for hours that afternoon. All the passion that had surfaced between Rose and Tom in the kitchen had ebbed away. The pair of them curled up, sleeping until dawn broke, all thoughts of dinner and sex forgotten.

## *Twelve*

It snowed on and off for a couple of weeks, so Tom continued to stay with Rose. Tom as a gardener couldn't work much in the winter months due the weather, and he always said when asked that it didn't matter to him where he lived. He retrieved his car from the village, and it had sat parked alongside the house for the best part of the month. He had all but moved into the house with Rose, just leaving random belongings in the flat over his brother's restaurant. Most of the stuff he needed or owned had found its way into the house. Every time he went back to the flat, he returned with another extra bag of stuff. Rose didn't know what to make of this change. It was subtle and unannounced but neither of them had brought the subject of living together up. It was as if they didn't need to discuss it, the situation was just evolving naturally, as things were wont to do in the house.

Rose had exhausted her flow of ideas and was hard at work being as practical as the weather would let her and taking every opportunity to sneak into her outbuildings and see if her ideas would work in the spaces she had to play with. Although there were random repairs needed in the majority of her outbuildings, most were fairly minor, some even cosmetic, and it was looking likely that her business plans might work. It was handy having Tom around to help her move some of the heavy stuff around. She had a barn full of old antique furniture, desks, chairs, cabinets, armchairs. She loved everything she had found so wanted to use it all. It was just a shame that the house was not big enough for her to fit it all into, but her plan was to use the furniture in the other buildings as there was ample space there. One of the outbuildings was used by Tom to store his garden tools and equipment in and there was space in another building that was big enough for him to park his work van in. Rose guessed that one of the buildings must have been an old coach house. The single-storey buildings alongside were obviously the old stables and the old barns could have been used for various farming purposes through the years. There was a separate building furthest away from the house, which was used by Steve, James, and George to store their trade equipment, they used part of it as office space too. It was an odd shape and had an external staircase to the upstairs. They only used the ground floor, leaving the upstairs empty.

Rose spent her time huddled over what they referred to as the 'captain's junk pile' in the coach house. The coach house was not very picturesque and certainly not very grand, but it seemed likely that coaches and horses would have been stabled in this building. Horses and coaches seemed very grand, and as the adjoining captain's house was anything but grand, it was something of an enigma. The junk pile was huge, and it was taking some time to sort through it all. Rose took her time, not forgetting that she had found the paintings that had caused so much trouble last summer in one of these buildings and they were expected to be extremely valuable. Too valuable for her to keep, she had donated them to the local museum/art gallery for the time being. She was happy to share these fabulous paintings with other locals and pleased not to have to worry about insuring them at home. She had listed them under her old aunt's name too, so they couldn't be traced back to the Captain's house by anyone who was not local to the area. The events of last year still played on her mind, making her extra cautious. She knew she needed to get someone to look at and value what she had unearthed on the ground floor. She planned to ask Geoff, the owner, and Phyliss, the manager of the antique shop in the village. A few days ago, Tom had found her a ladder to look upstairs when they had spotted a loft hatch. There was another big pile of stuff, covered in an old sail cloth as the previous occupants seemed to do with everything that they stored. Tom was going to secure the space for her, but they were going to leave that to another time so Rose could start planning and using the space downstairs in the meantime.

All of the buildings, except her house, were cold and draughty so it was not the best job for the winter months, but as she wanted some of the buildings to be used all year round and looking good, she knew she had to have a word with Steve again. He had helped her with making the derelict house her home and now she wanted him to help make the other buildings on her land into a business for her. He was a good builder and project manager and she counted him as one of her best friends. It was a little awkward when they met last year and, as their friendship had grown, she had sent unintentional mixed messages to Steve. It had turned out that Steve fancied her something rotten but was taking it slow. Tom reckoned he still did. Rose was treading very carefully with this friendship, as she had always had a very soft spot for Steve. Tom and Steve had always got on, because they were both nice guys at heart, but sometimes she would see a wry look on Tom's face if he caught her deep in conversation with Steve or sharing a joke. Steve always looked at Tom when he was with Rose with an incredulous look on his face, as if to say how on earth did you manage to snag her from right under my nose!

With the risk of upsetting Tom, she intended to ask Steve to work with her on her business plans. Tom wouldn't like her asking Steve to make her ideas and business plans come to life, he had offered his help to her already. She was happy to pay Steve for his expertise to keep it all on a business footing, she really didn't want to work in any way with Tom. He was her lover and another best friend. He was not and would never be her business partner. She knew that the time was coming when she would have to tell Tom, explain how she felt. She hoped he would not storm off back to his flat, leaving her alone again. Tom was like a pair of comfy slippers; she was getting used to his constant company and would miss him if he left. She desperately wanted to avoid this but was not sure if she could.

## *Thirteen*

It was a few days later when she realised that she couldn't put contacting Steve off any longer. One of the window frames was leaking in the old coach house, and the water was dripping onto the sailcloth over in the far corner. The snow had started to thaw and dripping could be heard from everywhere. As she had crossed from the house to the old coach house, she could finally see the cobblestones under her feet once more as the snow melted. Everything in sight seemed to be wet, not white anymore, and the *drip, drip, drip* was constant. She smelt the dampness first as she clambered over all the old furniture in her haste to have a look at the external wall and window of the coach house. She then saw the huge puddle of water pooling in the folds of the cloth that covered the furniture. She was not intending to look for the source of the leak at first, she was investigating the area as it lined up nicely with the stained-glass windows of the house.

She had all but forgotten the arrow that she had found while taking the Christmas decorations down on the upstairs landing, until Mickey had reminded her that morning over their regular morning tea and cake session. Mickey popped in most days, even when it had snowed hard, with his faithful hound Bert at his side. He was curious as to why she hadn't looked at the alignment before and this conversation had prompted her to clamber across the furniture to the external wall in the first place. He was even more curious as to why

# THE CAPTAIN'S FOLLY

she hadn't ventured up to the folly yet after she had made such a fuss on Christmas Day.

Rose loved the snow but didn't want to trek up to the folly in it. She was understandably nervous about the building, after hearing all the stories about how spooky it was up there in the winter months. The winter seemed to be the time when everyone she spoke to wanted to ask her about the Captain, the house, and the folly. Everyone wanted to know what it was like in the winter months, in the cold, dark, and wet. Her mum, dad, and friends were collectively pleased that Tom had moved in with her for the time being. 'It's not the place for a young girl like you to live alone' they all warned, 'especially in the winter when it's dark most of the time. You will end up as batty as your old aunt, you will. All up there on your own.'

The arrow and the alignment theory were overlooked once more as she haphazardly made her way back to an uncovered desk chair and pulled her phone out of the pocket of her jacket. She called Steve without even popping back to the house to tell Tom or even ask him what he thought. She knew she needed Steve, not Tom, to have a good look at all the buildings, she was so cross with herself for not checking that the buildings were watertight. She just assumed that they were. Tom stored his stuff on the other side of the building, as that side had been partially cleared by her mum and dad when they were looking for some garden furniture back in the summer. It was well used and always dry.

Her mum and dad had found a couple of table and chair sets and some reclining chairs for the garden in the same style as the bench in the garden. The garden furniture was grander than expected too, but there was far too much for the size of the garden. Rose admonished herself for not putting the garden furniture back under cover for the winter. She had left one of the tables outside because she wanted to use the table to feed the birds. She loved to see the birds perched on the table and made sure she had a stock of wild bird food, enough for the winter months. The table was next to the small ornamental tree that Mowzer couldn't climb, and the birds could retreat to if he ever got too close. Tom had told her the name of the tree, she was sure, but she could never recall it when asked. She liked to think it was brought back from overseas by her captain, as Tom usually exclaimed over the exotic, unusual array of the planting in her garden and always told her the names of these. The only tree that she could remember the name of was her Handkerchief Tree, the locals called it the ghost tree. Once a year the tree looked as if someone had tied little white hankies on it. It was very pretty, quite rare, and was her firm favourite. He was convinced that the Captain must have been one of the first plant hunters to travel the globe. Rose took a more romantic view that he bought flowers and plants back for his lady, a token of his love in the days when you couldn't pop down to the local shop or petrol station to grab a bunch of flowers when you wanted to please your girl or had done something wrong and needed to appease her instead.

She paced up and down waiting for Steve to answer and, just as his message started, Steve picked up. He knew it was Rose as his phone's settings always identified the caller.

Rose found that she was garbling into the phone instead of talking. Everything had gone so smoothly up until now and she had got complacent. Not being in the office or travelling into London she rarely had to sort anything out immediately anymore or react to any quick time changes. She knew how much her plans relied on a watertight workplace. She was thinking the worst and, after her hurried chatter, she was surprised to hear Steve's response.

"Rose, stop panicking about the water. Tom has already

mentioned that the wooden frames might need some repair, some of the tiles are loose and the doors into the coach house may need replacing or repair too. I have liaised with the conservation guy that we dealt with last summer and the job is in hand. We came down just before Christmas when you were away at Lisa's doing your Christmas shopping. The thaw will inevitably cause some problems because of the age of the buildings and the fact that they have never been touched, apart from the utility block that you renovated at the same time as the main house."

Rose gasped, stopped pacing, and drew a quick breath, "You mean you both discussed all of this without me, while I was away? Why with Tom? It's my bloody house, you know!"

"Tom knew you were undecided about your plans for the outbuildings and knew you wanted to take your time. We sorted out some of the roof repairs back in the summer so that his tools would be OK for the winter, the weekend you were at your mum and dads for a birthday, I think it was."

"So, this isn't the first time you discussed it and you have both been up on the bloody roof as well, without me knowing. Is there some big bill I am unaware of as well? Is there, is there?" she demanded.

"No bill, Rose. It was nothing really. I might need to bill you for the rest of it, but it shouldn't be too much. I can salvage most of the wood and bits from here and there. You have everything you need, right?"

Rose was so livid that she rang off. She threw the phone at the sailcloth, and it landed in the soft folds, thankfully, not hitting anything that was hidden underneath. She stalked out into the slushy yard. She pulled her hat out of her pocket and onto her head then she stuffed her hands into her pockets as she had no gloves and marched alongside the other buildings. When she came to the track at the border of her land, she turned, intending to go back to find Tom and have a right go at him. Steve's words replayed over and over in her head, 'You have everything you need, right?' and then she heard the exact same phrase in a different but familiar voice. 'You have everything you need right here', her captain had whispered, preceded by the phrase, 'Follow what you see.'

She took them both at their word and followed what she saw. Instead of heading back to the house, she turned onto the track and headed away from the house and everything in it. She needed to get away before her temper got the better of her, so she headed up the track, stomping through the slushy snow, kicking the icy snow drifts at the side with her feet as she went. Taking her temper out on everything she came across, she followed the track across the small bridge over the river and onwards across the land towards the marshes and the sea. She was taking the track to the folly, in a blind temper, without quite processing where she was going. She did think that she should tell Tom where she was going, but, in the moment, she was incapable of rational thoughts. Serve him right if he wondered where she had got to. She really didn't care.

The sky grew darker as she walked, and the temperature grew colder as she got closer to the folly. The track remained icy, and the snow was still deep. There was no thaw happening here. There were recent prints of a man and dog, she supposed, Mickey and Bert must have come along here for their afternoon walk. It was then she understood where she was and where she was going.

The thought of seeing Mickey and Bert calmed her down and she slowed her pace and started to walk normally. Her boots crunching on the snow as she walked, the snow encroaching to the top of her boots the further she got from the house and the nearer she came to the folly. She couldn't see Mickey, but she could hear Bert. He was barking. Short, sharp barks that sounded closer and then strangely faded out as if they were getting further away again. The barks had a sense of urgency to them. She had never heard Bert bark before as he wasn't a young dog and, although he was fond of playing ball, he was a solitary creature by nature. Her anger at Tom and Steve was replaced by a nagging sense of concern. Why was Bert barking? Why couldn't she hear Mickey talking to Bert as she expected he would if he barked at anything? Mickey loved a chat, and he would chatter to Bert in the absence of anyone else to talk to.

What on earth was going on?

## *Fourteen*

As she got closer to the folly, she noticed there were another set of footprints, quite a bit larger than Mickey's at the edge of the path. They looked like they were recent. She could see a large man walking in front of her along the track, his pace increasing like hers as the barking got more frantic. Bert sounded like he was in distress and with no discernible chat from Mickey to Bert, she was getting worried. Small shrubs and bushes obscured the final view of the folly from her and when she came back out into the open, she saw the stranger bending over Mickey, who was still and prone on the ground. Bert was really agitated now, his barks had turned to menacing growls and he was circling around his master anxiously. When Bert spotted Rose, he ran over to her and tugged at her jacket with his teeth, trying to physically pull her over to his master. She spotted his lead in the snow on the way, picked it up, and fastened it to his collar and held his lead tight, before speaking to the man to see what had happened to Mickey.

The man stood up on hearing her approach behind him and bellowed at her to call an ambulance at once. Because her hands had been in her pockets since she had left the coach house, she knew she didn't have her phone. She remembered she had thrown it away in temper before she had left. It was no use to her back there.

"I don't have a phone with me," she wailed to the man, who was crouched once more over Mickey. He turned and scowled at her and passed her his. The screen on his mobile phone was unlocked, and the camera option was still open. His gallery showed lots of recent photos of the folly and some of her outbuildings and house. She did not have time to wonder why he had taken photos of her property; she dialled for an ambulance and told the operator that she needed medical assistance to the folly. As she answered the many questions that were fired at her from the answering operator, it became apparent that there was no way an ambulance would be able to make it up the track. There was talk of an air ambulance or a stretcher. She handed the phone back to the man when they asked what was wrong with the patient for she still had no clue and Mickey had not yet moved or made a sound. She heard the man state that Mickey had a head injury that looks like he had fallen. He was unconscious when he arrived, she heard him say to the ambulance staff on his mobile

Rose should have been reassured by his presence and pleased that someone else was there to help her tend to Mickey, but she wasn't. Rose didn't like or trust this strange man that she had found with Mickey and Bert, who was still growling, albeit softly, didn't seem to take to him much either. She snatched the phone from him as he was about to end the call and asked the operator to call the police. The operator detected from her voice the reason why and informed her that the police had already been called and were on their way. The man left Mickey, loomed over her, and took his phone forcibly from her hands. Bert's growls turned into a snarl as he strained at the lead, seeking to protect her.

The man stood back, keeping well away from the snarling dog, and she took the opportunity to move across to where Mickey was lying unconscious on the ground. Rose and Bert sidled over to Mickey. Bert stood guard by his feet and Rose peered over his body to look at his face. The man was right. There was a large pool of blood forming at the side of his head. His breathing was shallow, and he was as pale as the snow he was lying on. Rose took off her jacket and laid it over his torso, pleased that she had worn the thickest jumper she owned this morning. She knelt in the snow and reached for his hand, holding it in hers, she looked back across at the stranger.

The man was dressed for the weather and could have afforded to give his jacket to Mickey rather than Rose. She wondered why he hadn't. He could have been exceptionally fat, but Rose suspected he was wearing lots of layers underneath his well-cut, full-length Barbour coat. His outfit was predominately brown and green with a solid pair of walking boots on his feet. He was dressed for countryside pursuits. Rose wondered if he carried a gun. He looked like he was the sort of man that liked blood sports. He was not a local, as Rose knew most of the locals by sight. He was not a countryside warden, neighbouring farmer, or landowner. He was an odd stranger who had offered her no explanation on what he was doing there. He didn't say much of anything or engage in any chatter. He glared at her and Bert, but his eyes softened with compassion when he looked at Mickey. His face was round, and he was wearing one of those deerstalker hats with the furry ear flaps, making him look like an overweight dog. His cheeks were ruddy, which could have been from the cold but more likely, Rose thought, from an alcohol habit. The more she looked at him, the more she disliked him. She was so glad she had Bert with her for protection, she mentally chided herself – how could she be so stupid to wander off without a phone? Or to tell a dodgy stranger that she was without one, in the middle of nowhere, as the snow blotted out the familiar landmarks around the folly itself which loomed over them, casting a shadow and making the late afternoon feel colder than it was.

Mickey stirred and started to mumble quietly. His breath was still very shallow. Rose let go of Mickey's hand and cradled his head in her arms as she sought to comfort him. Bert whimpered at his feet and crept up his body, resting next to his legs with his head on Mickey's stomach. Mickey's eyes flew open, meeting her eyes, he looked up at the folly and deep into her eyes again. He was trying to tell her something, she was sure. She looked up as he did and just saw a crow circling over the folly. The crow looked down at them and continued to circle ominously in the darkening sky.

## *Fifteen*

Typically, the police and the ambulance crew arrived together after what seemed to be a long time in the cold but was probably no more than an hour, during which time Rose ignored the stranger. She was normally a chatty person, but this man was oddly aloof, and she was sure he wouldn't welcome idle chit chat. Instead, she gave her full attention to Mickey who was drifting in and out of consciousness, trying to say something with his eyes every time he came round. He kept trying to focus on the sky and the crow still circling above, looking down, keeping its beady eyes on what was going on.

The ambulance crew took charge of Mickey and bundled him up on a stretcher and into the ambulance with a minimum of fuss and with total professionalism. The police officer who arrived at the same time was young, keen, and seemed to take a note of everything. Constantly asking direct questions. There was no messing about with him. He was very meticulous in his actions. Rose was extremely pleased that he was there and was able to take charge of the situation. She had felt very helpless and out of her depth with the whole situation. She was also very cold; her jacket was returned to her when the ambulance crew arrived and started to attend to Mickey, but it didn't seem to be making any difference to how cold she felt.

The man left the scene as soon as the police officer gave him permission to leave. He gave a curt nod at Rose as he left. He was eager to be on his way again, but he didn't continue along the track, he went back along the footpath towards the house, reminding Rose of all the photos she had seen on his phone of her properties, including the folly.

To her surprise she overheard the constable tell his control room that he was going to make sure Rose got home safely and all was well in the house. He had sensed her discomfort around the man and saw how upset she was about Mickey and was taking the time to look after her. After making the call, he said, "Will you be OK to take care of Mickey's dog? I can see the dog knows you well."

"Of course, I will," replied Rose, mentally seeing a picture of Mowzer's little face in her head and picturing his abject dismay. "I will be happy to look after Bert, but when I have warmed up, I really must go up to the hospital to see how Mickey is. What do you think happened to him?"

"I really couldn't say right now," the constable replied. "He may have just slipped on the ice, it is so slippery out here, but that cut looked nasty. Have you any idea what might have happened? It was lucky you both were out at the same time and came across him. You really shouldn't leave your mobile at home when you are out alone, especially on a day like this!"

Rose took the scolding about her phone with good grace, she knew it was a stupid thing for her to have done, she didn't enlighten the officer about the real reason she had left her phone at home – her temper. She just murmured her agreement that it was silly, and it was a good job that the man had a phone so they could call for help quickly. She wanted to ask loads of questions about the odd man, but she didn't really need to, as she had listened to the officer ask questions while the ambulance crew were dealing with Mickey. She just listened quietly while keeping herself busy with Bert, keeping the spaniel calm and making sure he didn't hinder the emergency workers so Mickey could get immediate medical attention and get on his way to hospital. She knew more about the man than she should. She had caught his name, Trevor, but missed his address as the wind had caught his words. The wind had taken bits of all the information that he had conveyed to the officer, but she knew enough. Enough to find out more about him and what he was up to.

All thoughts of leaky windows, the roof, or other repairs were overlooked as she worried about Mickey and the dodgy Trevor on the walk back to the house with the police officer. As Rose and the constable turned alongside the outbuildings, she saw Tom, accompanied by Steve, waiting for her. Tom had cleared what remained of the snow from the driveway and yard. He had also cleared her car from snow and defrosted the windscreen. Steve had his toolbox in his hand and was heading into the coach house. They both looked apologetic. Neither of them said a word, seeing as she was in the company of a uniformed police officer. Tom then stepped towards her and took her shaking hands in his, "Let's get you inside and warmed up. Is that OK, officer?"

"Yes, I will leave her with you, is that OK, Rose?" he asked.

"This is my boyfriend, Tom, and I will be just fine from here, thank you," she replied.

As he left, the officer handed her a card, printed with his details and the force logo along the top. He tapped the telephone number with his finger and as he did so he said, "Contact me if you need me. Or think of anything I might need to know. I will probably see you at the hospital as I do need to have a chat with Mickey."

Rose wanted to tell him about the photos she had seen and her gut feeling that Trevor was dodgy, but she knew this was not the time or place and she needed to focus on Mickey first.

## Sixteen

Tom got Rose inside, made her a warm cup of sugary tea and raced upstairs to run her a bath. She could smell the scent of her favourite bubble bath from downstairs. She wouldn't have time to soak in the bath as she wanted to get to the hospital straight away to see how Mickey was. She drank her tea sitting on the kitchen floor, cuddling Bert. She thought she was comforting Bert, but it was the spaniel that was comforting her, resting his head on her body at every opportunity and letting her stroke his long silky ears. She wished she could take him with her to see his master, but she knew the hospital would not let him in.

Before she went upstairs for a quick bath, she asked Tom to call Val and ask her to come over to sit with Bert in the house so he would not be left alone. She knew Bert would be fine on his own, but she wanted him to have company, not just be 'fine'. She also knew Tom would insist on coming with her to the hospital and she wasn't wrong. As soon as she was out of the bath and dressed, Tom appeared with his big outdoor coat on, ready to drive her to the hospital to see Mickey. Val was going to let herself in, as she had a spare key for the house. She would get there as soon as she could. She was happy to help. Rose suspected she would probably bring something for them to eat when they got in and a couple of slices of whatever cake she had just finished baking too.

When she arrived at the hospital, she explained that she was just a very good friend, Mickey had no family and she was looking after his dog, Bert. The police officer had already been to see Mickey. He told the nursing staff all about Rose and her relationship with Mickey, so they let her go up to the ward to see him. She was not allowed to stay long as visiting hours had long passed. She was allowed just a few minutes.

Rose hated hospitals. She found the all-pervading smell of the corridors and wards made her nauseous. She hurried along through the warren of corridors and side wards looking for her friend. She had passed the side ward where Mickey was and, on finding herself at a dead end, had to turn back. She didn't recognise her friend. One side of his face was covered with a huge purple bruise, and there were stitches in the gash on his head. His face was swollen and one of his eyes was hidden within the swelling. Poor old Mickey looked like he had been in the wars. When he saw Rose, he started to cry. Big silent tears slid down his cheeks and his body shook with emotion. He tried to form some words, but he was rendered speechless as the tears flowed. A nurse came running at the sight of his distress and looked at Rose accusingly. Mickey grabbed her hand and pulled her close before the nurse could send her away. He was surprisingly strong, and his fingers crept up and flexed around her wrist.

He whispered in her ear, "The crows are circling, trouble is near. That man was near, he was ... He is the ... trouble. He ..."

Mickey ran out of breath, took another intake of breath, and attempted to finish his sentence. The nurse gently pushed him away from Rose and stated quietly and firmly to Mickey, "That's enough now, you have to rest."

Bitterly disappointed and concerned for Mickey, Rose allowed the nurse to lead her away from Mickey but not before the nurse had settled him in bed, popping his hands back under the covers and telling him that he would be able to see Rose again tomorrow after a good night's rest.

She was none the wiser about what had happened, but relieved that he was safe and sound. There was nothing more she could do. Tom drove her home in silence. He knew that Rose was cross with him and Steve about the repairs to the outbuildings. He guessed that it was why she was out in the snow that afternoon, probably walking off her temper. He wanted to maintain the fragile peace for as long as he could, indefinitely maybe. But Rose wasn't thinking about Tom, Steve, repairs, or even her phone which was still in the coach house where she had left it. She was thinking about what Mickey had said to her about the crows, the trouble, the man – he must have meant Trevor. Her instinct had told her he was trouble the moment she saw him ahead of her on the path. What was he doing with all the photos of her property? Why were there so many? There was something about the actual photos that she had seen, they were at odd angles … just photos of roofs, bricks, tiles, windows. She had only recognised them because she knew them so well, most of the photos were of her buildings. None of the shots were of the whole buildings like any normal person would take if they liked a place. There was only one of the folly in the distance in the snow, perhaps he was taking a shot when Mickey fell. Or did he fall? Mickey hadn't told her how he got his injuries yet.

She looked across at Tom as they pulled up at the house. He looked so unsure of himself and worried. "There is no need to look so worried, Tom. Mickey is in the best place, and we're home now."

"I know that, Rose, I was worried about you and me as well as Mickey. Are you still cross?" Tom answered.

"I really don't know right now. It has been a long, stressful day. You might need to ask me in the morning when I have calmed down.

I really need to find my phone, I think I left it in the coach house earlier, will you come with me?"

Tom followed Rose as she got out of the car and walked across to the coach house. While they were at the hospital there had been a flurry of snow and the ground was covered with it once more. Rose could see recent footprints around the building and the door was slightly ajar. She nudged Tom and put her fingers on her lips, signalling him to stay quiet. There was dim light coming from the crack of the open door. She slowed down so Tom got to the door first and he opened it slowly. There was an almighty clatter as something fell to the floor inside the building. A squeal and then loud barking.

Bert threw himself out of the building into Rose and Tom, closely followed by Val brandishing a torch and shining it in their eyes.

"Val, it's us, silly. What are you doing out here in the dark?" Tom asked.

"It's a long story, but I heard these bells ringing and they got louder and louder and then stopped. This kept happening so I followed Bert, who led me here. It was daft coming out here alone with Bert in the dark, but Bert would not stop barking. I didn't know what else to do!"

Rose took the torch from Val, using the light to find the switch to turn on the electric lights in the coach house and pointed at her phone on the sailcloth covering the furniture. She then pulled a face as she realised that there was no way she could explain what it was doing in the middle of the big pile of furniture as it was obvious that she had slung it there. Tom raised his eyebrows at Rose and looked at the floor to cover his smile. Both Tom and Rose, it seemed, didn't want to share their earlier upset with Val, so Tom put her out of her misery and leapt across Val's view and deftly retrieved the phone from its resting place.

"How did that phone get there, my girl?" Val cried. "That's an impossible place to leave it. What's that got to do with the spooky bells I heard?"

"That's a long story that we need to share with you. Maybe two long stories, let's go inside and we can share. I fancy a cuppa," Rose said, looking at the phone display and seeing the time, "It's very late."

Then suddenly, they all heard, *Ting, Ting … Ting, Ting, Ting …*

The bells rang out. Everyone was silent, listening, including Bert, who brushed against Rose's legs and stayed glued to her, looking at Rose for reassurance. They all looked at each other as the bells continued to ring. The pitch getting louder, the bells getting louder before they stopped as suddenly as they had started.

Rose looked down at her phone. It was silent too.

## Seventeen

Val bustled around Tom and Rose when they returned to the house after leaving the barn. She had kept their dinner warm in the oven while they were away at the hospital. She served dinner, brewed them a pot of tea, and made sure they sampled some of her award-winning lemon drizzle cake before she had left, taking Bert with her to keep her company on the short walk back to The Lanterns.

She had some of his dog food at her house, as Mickey had stayed with her for a short while in the autumn while George, the local plumber, had fitted a new boiler in his cottage when his was beyond repair. Val had not wanted Mickey to be cold while the work was being done so he had stayed over with them. The annexe that Rose had stayed in last summer was unavailable as she had guests staying. Val hadn't charged him anything and loved fussing over him, treating him to home-cooked meals, cakes, and extra company in the evening.

Mickey could have visited a different person in the village every night as he was never short of invitations and offers. He was sorely missed by everyone since Doreen and Bob had closed and left the pub at the end of the summer, so he was not in his normal space, propped up at the end of the bar, with Bert snoozing at his feet. Mickey missed the companionship of the pub and the beer. He only had a half pint every night before switching to a soft drink or a coffee. He enjoyed a real glass of beer and enjoyed sampling the new brews. He was happy with just a taste. He was not an old soak or a raging alcoholic. Just an elderly, retired gentleman who enjoyed a drink in the 'boozer' with his mates.

As Val still had a big bag of Bert's food and a note of how much kibble Bert was allocated per meal, she had taken him home with her for the night and promised to return him in the morning, or if he didn't settle. Rose was certain that he would settle even if Val had to sleep next to him on the sofa. Val would let him sleep on the bed, but she was not so sure that her husband, David, would!

Tom had offered to walk Val home, but Val politely turned him down. She didn't want Rose to be in the house on her own after her experiences in the coach house, which had really unnerved her. She had always been a bit sceptical about the whole Captain's House scenario, not believing in ghosts or supernatural activities at all. Certainly not those that took place just down the lane from her place. She preferred to believe that the Captain's hat had been knocked off by a draught, the wind, or Mowzer being mischievous as he was very prone to be. Nothing spooky about the house at all. Just a series of unexplained events that if you thought about them rationally, they could always be explained. However, she was totally shaken by the recollections of Christmas that Tom and Rose had told her while they munched their dinner that evening. The mysterious bells and the handprints on the window. She totally needed Bert with her on the walk home. She was not going to call David as she would need to explain her change of heart about all things spooky and she wasn't ready to admit that to him just yet. She would never live it down if David got wind of it. Ever!

After Val had left, with Bert trotting along at her heels, hardly able to believe that he was getting another walk that day, Tom and Rose went straight to bed. They had talked everything out in front of Val when they came back from hospital. Rose had shared everything that had happened that afternoon, including the reason for her temper. Tom was relieved that it was all out in the open and that Val had been there to keep both their tempers in check so they didn't fall out over the unsolicited repairs that he had arranged with Steve behind her back, but with her best interests at heart. Val had acted like a mother hen, clucking over her errant brood and bringing them back into line with a crafty nudge with her sharp beak from time to time. She butted in when voices got loud, when emotions rose to the surface, and tapped them back down with some sensible words and well-meant advice. Rose was told by her mum never to go to bed on an argument, technically they weren't but they weren't feeling the 'love' either. She got under the covers and rolled one way and Tom got in and rolled the other way, keeping a big space between them in the middle.

That big space didn't last though, as Mowzer crept out from his sleeping position under the bed when he heard the bed springs announce 'company'. He launched himself with such a force between the pair of them that he made them jump in fright. Mowzer made himself cosy, ignoring their protests, and was purring loudly as Tom switched off the light. Mowzer continued to purr as Rose turned over and laid her arm on Tom's shoulder. His work was done. Satisfied with himself, Mowzer curled up tighter into a ball and continued to purr.

Peace descended on the house as the occupants slept soundly, thoroughly worn out by the events of the day. It was warm and cosy in the house, but outside was a different story. It was cold and frozen.

The moon was bright and casted a milky sheen on the frosted surfaces. There was movement everywhere in the courtyard. A mouse darted across the cobbles before the watchful eye of the barn owl perched on the roof of the coach house could see it. A badger emerged from its holt at the foot of the old oak tree alongside the footpath, keen to start its nocturnal wanderings. The first mouse was lucky, but the second mouse to venture into the yard from the coach house was not. The owl swooped down to catch his evening meal and disappeared into the night shadow.

Moments later, out of those same shadows stepped another figure briefly before they too disappeared into the night.

## *Eighteen*

It was just over a week later that Mickey was allowed to leave the hospital. He had tried to thwart his medical team a couple of days before. Although the hospital needed the bed, they wanted to make sure that Mickey was well before he was allowed to go home. The fall had left him a shadow of his former self, his confidence and cheekiness had been knocked out of him. He stated he felt like a teddy bear missing some stuffing and the 'growler' from his stomach. He didn't remember much about that afternoon anymore and when asked by Rose what he had meant by 'trouble', he rolled his eyes heavenward and muttered about something incomprehensible but always made reference to crows. Not just crows, magpies had been added to the mix. So bizarre.

Rose was so frustrated that Mickey could not remember what had happened and how he had ended up in the snow on his back with a head wound. Mickey was equally perturbed by all the fuss and the same question from Rose over and over again. Even though he loved company, he hated being the centre of attention and he was certainly that in the hospital. He couldn't fade into the background as he had a stream of anxious visitors from the village when word got round that he was hurt.

Mickey did not want to go home, but he didn't want to stay in the hospital either. He just didn't feel safe anywhere. He wished he could remember what had happened. He hoped he would feel safe when he had Bert at his side once more. Val had offered to have him stay at The Lanterns as long as he wanted or needed to stay. She had no guests booked until just before Easter, so he could stay with her until then. She had made up a guest room in the main house so he would feel more at home. Mickey had bartered for the annexe but was secretly pleased he would be with Val and David and not stuck out in the annexe on his own. Val had offered to keep walking Bert, with Rose taking turns too. Mickey was not well enough to walk Bert on his own, so was happy for 'the girls', as he called them, to take Bert out for him.

Bert didn't like going into the village or up the lane while Mickey was in hospital. His place was the folly and he pulled and whined to go that way up the footpath. Rose thought that in Bert's doggy brain he thought his master was still up there waiting for him, why else would he be so keen?

Rose was surprised when she had been pulled up the lane past her house and towards the footpath a few weeks later. Her shoulder and arm ached with the effort of trying to restrain Bert. All her cries of 'heel' were ignored, and his tail wagged furiously when he got to the footpath. She stepped in front of him and attempted to swivel him around to continue onto the village, but he looked up at her, using his big brown eyes to full effect in his handsome spaniel face. She paused for all of a nanosecond and then decided to let him have his way just this once and prepared herself to be pulled all the way to the folly. That was not the case however, as Bert, knowing he was going the way he wanted to, had miraculously stopped pulling and was walking like a show dog by her side. She felt his contact at every step she took, a little wiggle of his body brushing hers as he walked alongside her. He stopped every now and then to have a sniff at something unseen to her but interesting to him. She stood and looked around as he did so, keeping watch and feeling increasingly unsure as she got closer to the folly. The fact that Mickey had not told her what had happened, that he had forgotten, was not lost on her. She reached into her jeans pocket and checked she had her mobile phone with her this time. She never left home without it these days.

The snow had all but melted but the frost had remained in the shady areas. It felt very wintry the closer she got to the folly itself, as if the thaw had not yet reached here. The building seemed to loom over the surrounding marsh land, casting a shadow every which way, and the chill seemed to permeate right through her, into the very bones of her. The building which looked almost pretty and fairy-like in the summer was starkly contrasted by its menacing presence in the winter months, even in broad daylight.

Bert sat quietly at her feet when she arrived at the foot of the folly tower. He had expected Rose to let him off for a run around like his master did, but Rose did not know this part of his routine. She needed him close by and he seemed to understand this. When she saw the bench tucked away by the trees she sat down with Bert at her feet. The bench was placed at an odd angle to the building, so you could see for miles towards the sea and back towards her house. She remembered Mickey saying how you could see right out to sea on a fine day from the top of the folly's tower.

The crows started to circle the tower as she sat down, they floated high in the air on the thermals and then drifted lazily towards her, swooping down and then rising but always circling the tower. The black crows in the grey skies, the muddy path, the trees bereft of leaves in the wintertime all blurred together as she watched the crows. She watched them as they circled closer and closer to the grey blocks of stone that formed the folly behind her. She turned to look at where they were going. As she turned to see, they vanished.

Everything that was familiar vanished. All that remained was the folly and as she turned around the scenery remained the same. She caught the arm of the bench as she turned back around to check on Bert, but he had disappeared too and was no longer at her feet. She could no longer see her feet; they had vanished too. She felt a breath on her cheek and the familiar tones of her captain as he whispered urgent words into her ear, she strained to hear what he was saying but it was all intelligible, incomprehensible, apart from one word: 'beware'.

## Nineteen

She sat very still and waited.

Waited until she stopped panicking that she had lost everything around her that was familiar. She wanted to scream a visceral scream that was bubbling up from her stomach. She gripped the arm of the bench and the edge of the seat below her thighs, relieved that her legs were still solid and feet firm on the ground. His whisper was incessant in her ear and its tone increasing in urgency. The speech was incoherent apart from one word, 'beware'. The intonation of that word 'beware' was clear. Very, very clear. Nothing else was. The bench shuddered slightly as she felt someone sit down, close enough for her to feel their thigh against her own. Their shoulder lightly bumping alongside hers. Their breath on her cheek. She surmised it was her captain, noting her unease and using all of his strength to comfort her as well as warn her of whatever he was saying she should 'beware'.

As she shifted her weight and sought a glimpse of her captain, the breath on her cheek quickened and she felt a warm gush of air with a dampness that wasn't there before. She blinked and a pair of brown eyes blinked back. Familiar brown eyes set in the spaniel face of Bert, who proceeded to clamber into her lap and snuggle up into her body. He wiggled and fussed. Eager to be very close. She hugged him, pleased he was with her once again, but she couldn't help but wish that she had her captain at her side again. Bert pressed his face close to hers, sniffing her intently and then sniffed at the surrounding air. He jumped off her lap and started to growl quietly then loudly. His hackles rose as he got louder and louder till his growls were punctuated by barks. Short, sharp barks.

She jumped off the bench and knelt next to Bert, looking in the same direction to see what was making him bark. A pair of walking boots could be seen moving behind a couple of shrubby trees that were growing alongside the building. There was not much space there and no discernible path to follow. Talking softly to Bert, she edged him closer to the tree line to get a closer look. This was her land and the building belonged to her too. As she moved it crossed her mind that it might be a walker seeking a discreet place to have a wee, but that didn't matter, she thought. If they were disturbed having a 'wild wee', it would serve them right for tiddling up the side of her building. How dare they! She squeezed between the shrubby trees and the heavy odour of aftershave assailed her nostrils. It was a heavy, thick scent. A scent her dad would use on a night out. She knew it and had smelt it before, the last time she was at the folly when she found Mickey after his accident. It was not Mickey's, he wasn't the type to wear aftershave and it couldn't have been the nice policeman's – he was too young for this aftershave as it was an eighties' scent. The medical men that helped with Mickey smelt of cleanliness and sanitisers. It had to be Trevor. The scent personified him. His age. His dress sense. Everything.

Why was he creeping around the folly building, tucked out of sight in the trees, sneaking and poking around? What was he up to and was she safe? All those thoughts raced around her head as she tried to silence Bert so she could watch to see what he did and where he went. It was far too late. Trevor pushed past her and out of the undergrowth, nearly knocking her off her feet. He stumbled and slipped, his expensive walking boots not doing much to keep him upright. As he reached the open land next to the bench, he took off his deerstalker hat and wiped his face with his gloved hand before replacing it on his head. He looked thoroughly scared.

The fact that he looked so scared made Rose suddenly confident that she could deal with him, with her trusty sidekick, Bert. For he was literally at her side as if he was glued to her leg, looking as formidable as he could with his head held high above his rigid body. Jaws open wide. showing his teeth. Rose pushed her way back out of the undergrowth, startling Trevor, who didn't look as if he was aware that she was there too.

He seemed to have shrivelled in size since she last saw him, not so plump and pompous. He didn't look so sure of himself either. Rose saw that he still had his phone glued to his hand like the last time she saw him and wondered if he had been taking more photos while skulking about in the undergrowth. He didn't look embarrassed, so she surmised that he wasn't having a wild wee as she had supposed. She suppressed a grin and kept quiet, so Trevor had to speak first. She wanted to shout and bluster, to scream and shout about rights of way and not messing about with what wasn't yours, but sensed that the time wasn't right, and neither was Trevor. He seemed to be staring at the gap in the undergrowth from whence he had come. The undergrowth was trodden down so he had obviously been that way before. Had he knocked Mickey over the same way he had almost taken Rose off her feet, was this what happened up here that day? She knew that this was ridiculous as Trevor was in front of her on the track toward the folly that day and they had both found Mickey together, or had they? There were other footprints on the track that day, Trevor could have doubled back to cover his tracks.

Trevor broke the silence, "It's you again. Was it you a moment ago, was it you last time? Are you deliberately trying to send me mad? What is it about this place? Surely up here I should get peace and quiet, why do I keep hearing those bloody bells?"

Rose was just about to reply that she couldn't hear anything when she heard the faint sound of bells in the distance. Just faintly, every now and then. She pointed into the distance towards the sea and replied, "Those bells from far away. Are those what you mean?"

"Of course, but they are right here," he whined, grabbing both ears through his hat and shaking his head vigorously, looking to all intents and purposes like a mad bloodhound, "so, so loud, right in my bloody head. I don't get what's wrong with this bloody place. The sooner I can turn it around, the sooner I will get rid." With that he stomped off, completely disregarding Rose, without the apology or chat she was expecting. Or at the very least a 'Hello' and surely asking after Mickey.

Was he the 'trouble' that she was being warned about? She pondered as she followed him back down the track towards home with Bert at her side. She vowed to find out and bring Tom up here to help her discover what he was up to. He was obviously up to no good, but what was it and how did it connect to her folly?

# Twenty

It took Mickey a good few weeks to get back on his feet.
Val and David had loved having him as a house guest and 'the girls' had really enjoyed their walks with Bert. But after the events of that day, Rose always turned the other way from Val's place so she was not tempted to go back up to the folly on her own.

She had not managed to persuade anyone to join her to go back up to the folly yet. She wasn't entirely sure why she did not have the courage to go up there again on her own after her weird encounter with Trevor. It was so unlike her, to get so rattled.

As the weather had cleared along with the snow, it seemed that every man she knew in the area had swarmed like a crowd of busy bees around the cluster of her outbuildings. Steve had called upon all his friends in every trade, who popped in before and after their current jobs and were busy fixing everything that he and Tom had noticed before Christmas. The lights blazed late into the evening and Rose felt like she was living in an episode of one of those design and renovation programmes on the TV. She almost expected to see George Clarke, her favourite TV celebrity, knocking a hole out of one of the walls to make a bigger, workable space. This was wishful thinking on her part as she fancied him rotten. She had lots of space and lots of things to clear too. She was expecting a visit from Phyliss to have a look at what she had unearthed and give her some valuations before she used some of the furniture for her new business venture.

Rose never expected her utility room to be so well used. She hadn't wanted to change the layout in her galley-type kitchen in the house or modernise it in any way. To get round this she had put as many modern appliances as possible in the nearest outbuilding instead, just a short hop across the yard. Rose spent her time making tea for everyone before she turned her new utility area over to the boys to use for making their own refreshments. She suspected there was a lot more beer and lager being consumed in the evenings than tea or coffee! She wasn't sure she should let them in there as she felt that it was her space, but, as she suspected, no one touched her dirty undies, let alone washed and popped them in the tumble drier for her. On the draining board and sink stood their mugs, some were washed but some, by the colour on the inside of the mug, had only ever been rinsed in their life. Rose was pleased to have the company and it felt like she was getting the business side of things kickstarted at last. Her long list of new year's resolutions was finally getting ticked off.

As Mickey felt better, he started to reminisce about the pub and how the village needed a focal point to get together. Rose was not entirely surprised when she first spotted Mickey from her kitchen window turn the other way, heading for the door of her utility room instead of her back door. Bert was trotting along as always at his side. Mickey had returned to his little cottage as soon as he felt well enough, walking Bert back along the lanes to herself and Val every day for company. He timed his walks to coincide with lunch and dinners and both herself and Val made extra for either the freezer or to dish up for Mickey to join them. He didn't go out early like he used to and had not ventured back to the folly since his accident. Rose really wanted to ask him if he remembered what had happened that afternoon yet, but Tom urged her to let Mickey tell her in his own time. Mickey was quieter than usual and not so full of his usual bluster and tall tales. He always returned home before dark if he was alone and on foot. Tom and David would run him back to his cottage in a car if it got too late.

It sounded like there was a party going on when Rose opened the door to the utility room to see what Mickey was up to. Most of the men were packing up and having a last beer and chat before leaving. The lively chat could be heard across the yard and, as she entered, she heard the punchline of what she assumed to be a very rude joke. The guys looked sheepish and hot under the collar as she stepped into the room, but Mickey roared with laughter at their discomfort and was looking more like his old self. Not perched on a bar stool in the corner but on one of her kitchen stools instead. Steve followed her into the room and raised his hands, gesturing for quiet.

"Scaffolding is going up at The Ship, looks like the new owners have had their planning permission approved for the apartments." He looked around with a grin. "This place is not big enough and Rose won't let us use it for ever, what are we going to do now?"

## Twenty-One

The village had been in an uproar ever since they had realised that The Ship was not going to be a pub anymore. This might have been the reason why Bob and Doreen had not returned to the village for Val's Christmas Party. Rose had spoken to Doreen a couple of times since they had left the village and Doreen had told her that it was no use the villagers being sorry once they had gone. They should have spent more time and money in the pub while it was there. They didn't want to leave but the pub wasn't making enough money for them to stay. Doreen was nagging Bob to move back into The Ship once it was converted into swanky luxury apartments and was hankering for the top-floor apartment with an additional roof terrace added for a glimpse of the sea, but Bob wanted to stay far away from the scene of his business disaster in their rented cottage miles away.

It was strange really that Rose had got on better with Doreen since she had left the village. The 'painting incident' was never mentioned, forgotten really, and Rose felt she had a steady ally in her new friend. She hoped she would come back to visit and was going to ask Doreen if she wanted to use the shared studio space for her new business. She was upcycling old furniture. She hadn't sold the contents of the pub with the property, and she was busy painting the tables, chairs, bar stools and the like in bright jazzy colours or muted tones and selling them on with a massive profit. Doreen didn't seem to be settled where she had ended up on the outskirts of the neighbouring village. It was close as the crow flies but, in reality, was miles away using the lanes that crisscrossed the marshland and the fields of sheep pasture which adjoined the marsh. Rose hoped she could persuade Bob to relocate at least closer and the draw of affordable studio space might entice them back in the right direction.

She already had a few people in mind to approach who might be interested in using the shared studio space she was creating. There were a couple of large spaces that had lots of natural light, and with the addition of workbenches and a large table in the middle they would be ideal for art and craft-type work. Rose didn't want to post an advert unless she really had too. She would love to create a busy workspace full of people she knew that she already liked and respected, but she was not daft enough to think that this was feasible or realistic. She was going to do her very best though. She had had Ashley on her initial list, who had printed the wrapping paper that Mickey had wrapped her Christmas present in. Sue, a local artist, who exhibited in the local museum and shops, making a tidy sum selling local landscapes and botanical art to visitors. Tilly, Joe's girlfriend, who worked in a florist in town and wanted to start up her own business but had no premises.

She had got the guys to portion off one of the buildings into separate office spaces, planning to rent a few out on a casual basis and have permanent spaces for others. She planned to ask Dennis, the local photographer who worked alongside Tilly most weekends covering local weddings between them, if he needed office space or somewhere to meet clients from time to time.

She had loved the hustle and bustle of all the workmen descending 'en masse' to work on her outbuildings. She was fortunate that Steve had managed all the work for her, making it a largely cost effective and positive experience for her. Steve had made a point of addressing her if he found any issues that needed a definitive decision, not speaking to Tom at all. Her recent assertiveness was not lost on the pair of them, and they were tiptoeing around her for most things.

Mickey loved all the company too and propped up the utility worktop most mornings like he used to prop up the bar at old defunct pub. If Rose wanted a cuppa and chat, she had to go and find him now as he dropped in there instead of coming to her in the house. She hoped he was not avoiding her but suspected that he was missing the male companionship of the pub as much as the rest of the guys.

There was another pub not too far away, along the seafront. The Seahorse. This bore no relation to The Ship, albeit it was another licensed premises. It had been modernised within an inch of its life and usually catered for the tourists and not the locals. However, some of the younger locals of The Ship had already transferred their allegiance to the new pub. It stocked trendy craft beers, always had good music, and had recently started to invite local bands to play there, picking up the local bands and some extra income after The Ship had closed. They only invited the younger bands, not the older bands that were popular at The Ship, which alienated the likes of Mickey. George and James were regulars at the new 'local' and were enjoying their bands new popularity at the 'Horse', as they affectionately called it, dropping the 'h' depending on how drunk they were and who they were talking to. If anyone well dressed came into the pub while they were playing, they always thought it was a talent scout and made sure to talk to them before they left. They were constantly teased for this habit as most of the well-dressed folk were bankers and office workers stopping for a drink before going home to the family. The men making sure their kids were well and truly asleep and the bedtime routine firmly finished before rocking up at home. The road that ran along the seafront was a popular route with locals and visitors alike. Traipsing up and down the narrow lanes was not popular with anyone and anyone following their sat nav with a wide car usually found out quite swiftly that the lanes needed to be navigated with care.

## Twenty-Two

The identity of the buyer of The Ship was a mystery. A London property services company was listed as a contact, but despite all the locals wanting to find out who was behind this façade, everyone came up against a dead end. This looked dodgy to most people and made the villagers speculate over the slightest detail. The guys that had congregated in Rose's utility room and had been working on her outbuildings were particularly interested as they were all hoping to be asked for a quote and have another job to go to when her job was finished. The village was holding its collective breath waiting to find out what was in store for one of their cherished buildings. Anyone who attended the building in an official capacity had been told not to disclose the nature of the work and appeared to be just wandering around making notes and taking calls. Phyllis, the manager of the antique shop, had taken to walking her little poodle, Porridge, up and down the street, practically walking his little legs off, while she tried to eavesdrop on what was being said in conversation on 'site'. The swanky apartments were in progress, but it was all a bit 'behind closed doors' for everyone's liking. No one local was in the know at all.

The street was always very busy with people idling and walking dogs, gossiping at front doors but all eyes were on the old pub and there was a race to be the first to know who was behind these apartments and if there would be any unforeseen implications to the village.

Rose was as curious as the next person, maybe more so as she knew from her property deeds that her land bordered with theirs and that the history of both properties seemed to be mixed up together. Although the details of the old tales had died out with time, the events of last year had highlighted that even if the stories weren't remembered, history had a way of catching up with the present.

She did not object to the planning requests, partly because she was tied up in her own plans for her own future, but also because she was happy that someone had bought the property and it was not going to be one of those sad derelict pubs, just boarded up and forgotten. It was in the heart of the village so, when Doreen and Bob left, it seemed to have left the village with the sense that someone had ripped the heart out of it. Never more so than at Christmas when the pub was usually a blaze of colour with Christmas lights and a big Christmas tree outside. The windows were always lit with lamps during the winter months, even if the pub was closed, just low wattage orange lamps on every windowsill. The pub had been a key feature of the village as long as everyone could remember and was never dark. It was never as aloof as it was now, covered with plastic sheeting and scaffolding. The old pub façade gone.

Rose wondered whether she should have thought of a hospitality business plan – a coffee shop or wine bar, to keep her afloat. She had the customers by default as her outbuildings seemed to be the new meeting place for most of the workman who stopped to have a chat and a drink while they were there. Her friends tended to pop over there first before coming to see her, to see what was going on and whether anything was finished. Mickey seemed to be always in attendance these days, but Christian, the original occupant of the outbuildings when she first arrived, was conspicuous in his absence. No one had seen him for months, it looked like he had found somewhere else to live for the winter months now Rose was living there. He wasn't at his boat on the shore, which had been lying untouched. She hoped he was OK and often asked Steve or Tom if they had seen him in their wider travels for work.

## Twenty-Three

The weather brought another icy blast to Kent just when everyone thought they had seen the back of winter. They had enjoyed a brighter, slightly warmer weekend with no frost which made everyone think of sunnier days to come. So, it was a rude awakening when Rose woke up to a heavy frost and a white dusting of snow outside. She had been busy with her plans while the guys had been busy on her outbuildings and had popped a card about the business spaces for let in the local shop window several weeks ago.

Although Rose could have posted on the village or the local business Facebook accounts, she chose not to. She knew that most of the village were spending their spare time loitering outside the village shop to keep an eye on the renovations of The Ship apartments and had their ear to the ground for gossip as to who had bought it. It made sense to put a brightly coloured card in their view, to give her potential 'customers' something else to think about as they pondered about the demise of their beloved pub. Tantalisingly, the ground floor of the old pub was not going to be used for accommodation and was still going to be used for 'business/commercial' use. Its windows were now covered over with newspaper on the inside and no one had an inkling of what it was going to be. Rose worried that it was going to be used for the same use as her outbuildings and that she might have her first local competitor already.

The village had never been busier. The premises of the vets and groomers were not far from the old pub either and the animals of the village had never been so well cared for and pampered. Everyone was using any excuse to pop into the village and have a look at the developments. Rose was guilty of this too and had developed a habit of going out in the morning for a newspaper. When she lived and worked in London, she bought the Kindle version of the newspaper to read on the train. A different newspaper every day. Now she popped along to the shop with everyone else in the village. She was in the habit of buying the newspaper that looked the most interesting, had the most intriguing headlines or interesting articles, but only after she had flicked through every newspaper in the shop. She loved village life and chatting to everyone. People were now referring to her by name, instead of 'the young lady from the Captain's House down the lane'. She still batted daily questions from the locals asking if the place is still haunted and people continued to tell her of their regular glimpses of her ghostly captain in the front windows of the house when they passed.

It was nearly lunchtime when she arrived for her morning newspaper, and she immediately noticed that her card was missing from the window. In its place was a cute little poster advertising a cake sale and tabletop sale for the local animal rescue charity. Disappointed, she marched to the counter without browsing the newspapers as usual. Dotty, manning the till, saw her approach and rummaged around underneath the till and produced her card.

"You paid for a month, my dear," she said, "do you want to pay for another month?"

Feeling guilty that she had thought that anything was amiss, Rose replied, "Of course, I do, no one has contacted me about wanting to hire some space. Perhaps no one is interested."

Dotty looked down at the card and handed it back to Rose. "You should have made your contact details a little clearer. It is hard to read it as you have added bits."

Rose looked at the card, now in her hands, and squeaked in dismay. Her card had been altered. Her email address had been amended, a few extra letters had been added and her mobile number had been rendered illegible. The ink was the same and an attempt had been made to match her writing style. Someone had sabotaged the card advertising her business. Who and why would someone do that?

Dotty saw her expression change and saw her dismay. Dotty was fairly new to the village as well. You had to have lived in the village for many years to be classed as a local. She worked in the shop in the mornings after the school run until lunchtime. She was a busy mum of two children, who went to the village school.

"Rose don't even go there, it's not a problem. I know exactly who has looked at that advert over the last month. I knew most of them as they are regular customers like you. Give me a second and I will write a list of the names for you. I know most of their addresses and I can collect their mobile numbers for you when they next come in. Stop worrying, we can sort this."

"I know we can, but who would do such a thing and how did they manage to take the card, alter it, and pop it back without anyone noticing? Really odd and kind of worrying, don't you think?"

Dotty shrugged her shoulders and pulled a face. She grabbed a stool from behind the counter and put it beside hers and motioned Rose to sit by her side. Within a few minutes she had produced a list and between them they had worked out why they would have wanted the space in her outbuildings.

The list contained:

Ashley, who printed textiles, paper, and painted watercolours.

Sue, who painted local landscapes and botanical art.

Tilly, the florist and Joe's girlfriend.

Dennis, a professional photographer.

Pearl, a home baker and caterer.

Rose knew precisely who to ask first. She had met Tilly and she had her mobile number already. She dialled straight away. Tilly's recorded message answered her call stating that she couldn't talk right now as she was busy. Of course, she was, Rose concluded; it was shop hours after all. She was pleased that the phone wasn't answered as she realised that she could have dropped Tilly in it with her boss as she was currently working in a florist shop in town. Her boss probably wasn't aware of her other plans. She left a message asking Tilly to call her back later.

She looked back at the card in her hands and saw it just had her name, not the location or any Captain's House references. She was just about to ask Dotty for another card to complete and saw that Dotty had already slipped a new one on the counter in front of her with a pen alongside.

She carefully wrote out another card making the heading 'The Captain's House' and underlining it in red ink from the red pen which had been handed to her by the attentive Dotty. She printed her name, mobile number, and email address underneath and the overview of the premises available to let. She took a photo of the finished result with her phone. Dotty and Rose exchanged conspiratorial glances and then Dotty marched over to the window and put it back in its rightful place, shoving the poster over a bit to make room.

After thanking Dotty profusely for all her help and buying her daily newspaper, Rose left the shop and wandered home deep in thought. Who would do that and what would they stand to gain from it? Did she have an enemy in the village that she was unaware of?

# Twenty-Four

Rose was washing up her dinner dishes at the kitchen sink and saw Tilly's car park up next to the outbuildings. She opened the door wide to welcome her indoors out of the cold air that was threatening to snow again. There had been snow flurries on and off all afternoon. Tilly had not visited the house before and Rose was sure that she had been looking for an excuse to pop over for some time. She was right. Tilly was on her way to Joe's for the evening to spend time with him on one of his rare nights off from his restaurant, but popped into Rose on the off chance, so she said. She went on to say, "I can't stay long but wanted to speak to you in person as I guess from the message you left me on my mobile that you want to talk about the card in the window."

She had time for a cuppa with Rose though, as almost everyone did in the village. She took her coat and hat off at the door and leaned against the door jamb as Rose boiled the kettle and made the tea. They took the tea into the back room and sat down. Tilly looked around in astonishment at the quality of the bookcases and the window seat. She stretched her hands out to the fire roaring in the grate and announced, "It's all true, you have an amazing little house, what a shame you have to share it with the infamous ghostly captain, eh!"

Once Tilly had got the ghostly vibes and chatter out of her system, Rose prompted her to talk about the card.

Tilly said, "I took a photo of the card in the window on my phone when I nipped into the shop to get some snacks on the way to Joe's last week. He is really snobby about what he eats, and I had a hankering for some ready salted crisps. The ordinary ones, not the expensive sea salt and black pepper, triple and double cooked extra puff ones or such that he gets ... just normal, standard ones. I always treat myself to something when I am passing that shop as they sell all my favourites. I eat them on the way to his. Don't split on me, Rose, as I really like him, I pretend that I like all his kind of stuff. I even told him that I was on a healthy eating kick, but that just meant that he started roasting his own crisps for me in some weird healthy oil. Totally backfired on me that did, and I am a size six, so there is no chance of him believing I am on a diet, is there?"

Rose giggled. "Have you still got the photo?" she asked.

"Yes, I kept it as I was meaning to call you but, when I did, the number was unobtainable and didn't connect. Joe said I should email you instead, but I haven't got round to that as I have been so busy. Joe did notice that you had corrected the card and said that it wasn't like you as you were so methodical and would have started again if you had made a mistake. We told Tom and he was going to get you to change it properly. I guess he forgot to tell you."

"Tom knew about the corrections on the card and he never told me? How strange. That's not like him, is it?" Rose replied.

"No, it's not like him, but it didn't seem important as he checked your email address and Tom thought that if people didn't get through on the phone that they would leave a message instead. He was going to mention it to you when he saw you next, I suppose it slipped his mind."

Tilly passed her phone to Rose with the photo displayed, it showed an extra number in her phone number, but her email was correct.

Even odder, as the card that Dotty handed her today that was previously displayed showed her email altered as well. Rose still had the card folded in her jeans pocket, she stood up and fished it out. After a quick glance she handed it to Tilly. There were extra letters and numbers squeezed into her email address, rendering it totally wrong. No wonder no one had contacted her. They couldn't have done so if they tried.

Tilly swilled the last of her tea around the mug in her hands and swigged the dregs. "I totally agree, very odd. At least you have it all sorted now," she said as Rose handed her the list that Dotty had made earlier. "I know most of the people on this list, I will give them a call for you tomorrow when I get some time during the day."

She gave Rose a quick hug on her way out, then she was gone, putting her coat on as she went out of the door and pulling it tightly around her as she got into her car. Rose wondered if she was going to call into the shop for snacks on her way to Joe's.

How odd, the email address being correct, then that being changed too. Whoever did it, had to have done it on two separate occasions without being seen. It seemed malicious. As she returned from the kitchen to the comfort of the fire and her tea, she wondered why Tom hadn't mentioned it to her. He was not mentioning a lot of things these days. Mowzer jumped up on her lap and rubbed his face into hers, sensing her uncertain mood. She leaned back into the chair, giving him room to curl around on her lap and resting her mug on the arm of the chair with one hand, the other hand stroking his fur gently, she gazed into the embers and wondered who it was and why would they be messing with her? Why her?

## Twenty-Five

Rose did not get a chance to talk to Tom before the weekend. Tilly had worked her magic and called everyone that had appeared on Dotty's list. Tilly updated Rose the following day. Some of them had already tried to contact Rose and several were still thinking about it. Rose was so pleased that she didn't have a direct competitor who had identical premises close by for her potential clients to deflect to when she had proved difficult to contact, but she was still perturbed by the alterations. She really didn't like the fact that someone disliked her enough to try to ruin her fledgling business at this early stage.

Rose thought that there might have been plans for co-working spaces on the ground floor of the old pub. As it was in the centre of the village, it would have really scuppered her plans.

It was still a mystery to everyone what that downstairs area in The Ship was going to be. All the work seemed to be on the apartments and residential areas and the ground floor was sitting empty and being used as a thoroughfare and dumping ground for the workmen. It was sad to see and more than once Rose caught Mickey peering around the main door of the pub, staring wistfully where his bar stool would have sat, when she popped in the shop for her daily newspaper.

Tilly was keen to rent some space in her newly renovated buildings, she already had some savings and business plans drawn up and ready to go. She just needed to take the 'leap of faith' and hand in her notice at the shop where she had worked since she had left school. Tilly was setting up a floristry business mainly catering for weddings and corporate events, not funerals or other special occasions. She wanted to specialise and compliment the floristry businesses in the area, not take any business away from her first employer. The Captain's House was far enough away Tilly hoped not to impact too much on her business. She had always wanted to be her own boss. Tilly was a forthright but introverted individual, who disliked being on show in the shop and never liked not knowing who was going to walk through the door. She was looking to create her own business online, so she could dictate how the business worked on her own terms and decide which jobs suited her. She could focus on the flowers and not have to waste time chit chatting to the customers who only came into the shop for a chat. She was looking forward to focusing solely on her floristry skills and not the day-to-day dynamics of the shop.

Tilly had called Rose several times in the week to chat over her business plans and support Rose with hers. Their friendship was initially based on business and the fact that they were both dating brothers, but it was developing into something more tangible. Rose found herself discussing Tom with Tilly. Tilly agreed with her that he was becoming more distant lately with everyone and that she and Joe rarely saw him even though he lived in the apartment above the restaurant. Very strange. Rose was hoping it was nothing to do with her. Every relationship has its ups and downs, and although their relationship was still fairly new, she was sure they were both happy. They only seemed to squabble over the house as Tom seemed to get involved with bits without telling Rose what he was up to. Rose could feel her doubts coming back. Did he want her for the house and garden, or would he still love her without everything that came with her?

She was pleased she had a list of interested people, so she didn't have to meet them one by one. She had plenty of time to play with and could have managed individual chats, but she decided to contact everyone on the list and suggest an open day for them all to visit, to get to know each other and wander around at their leisure instead. She would greet them and meet them afterwards. People could get a feel for the place then and she would get a feel for how it would work and how to split the spaces further should she need more or less. She was going to leave the card up in the window to give it a few more weeks to run, just in case anyone else was interested. She was also going to call Doreen too and invite her over for the day to have a look.

The thought of an open day instead of the original plans she had discussed with Tom highlighted the differences that were growing between them. She shrugged her feet into her welly boots and bundled up against the weather, which was still constant snow showers. She wandered up the lane to see if Val was in. She needed a chat, woman to woman, as Val had known Tom from a boy. He referred to her affectionately as 'Auntie Val'. She was almost at The Lanterns when she heard a car being driven fast behind her. She expected to hear it slow down when the driver saw a pedestrian, but they didn't slow down at all. The road was clear, but still icy in places, it was irresponsible to drive that fast in such conditions. The driver didn't seem to care, or they were running late. Rose dived into the hedge in fright when she realised that the driver was not going to slow at all to pass her. If they had seen her at all. Luckily, she was bundled up in her winter clothing and heavy winter coat so that the hedge was just uncomfortable rather than painful. The hedge would have ripped her to shreds if it had been the summer. From the hedge she watched a chunky Mercedes-type car accelerate away. The driver didn't even check in their rear-view mirror that she was all right.

Shaken but not hurt, she continued on her way to Val's, berating herself that she had not thought to look at the registration number of the vehicle. She was too busy keeping herself safe. She was sure that she would recognise the car again, it had a silver logo on the back of the vehicle … that was all she could remember.

Was this just an unfortunate incident or was someone out to hurt her too?

## Twenty-Six

When she arrived at Val's she was still picking bits of ivy and branches from her coat. The sleeve was torn slightly. She was not upset that the coat was torn, totally the opposite, she was very pleased she had worn it and it wasn't the summer when she would have been wearing shorts or a summer dress and it would have been her arms and legs that would have been scratched and sore.

Val opened the door almost straight away, as she was prone to do. She prided herself on her Bed and Breakfast business and she was expecting some guests that afternoon so had been listening out for them. She had divulged to Rose that her guests tended to turn up whenever suited them, no matter what the time of arrival was stated on the particulars. She had the uncanny knack of always knowing exactly when they would arrive; she always seemed to have the kettle on the boil and freshly baked scones ready to go. Seeing Rose looking so dishevelled on her doorstep was a big surprise, as she was not expecting Rose to call that afternoon.

She quickly enveloped Rose in a big hug. Hustling her straight through to her kitchen at the back of the property, she sat her down in a big squishy armchair and brought her a fresh cup of tea after lacing it with several teaspoons of sugar. The typical British remedy for a bad experience or shock. She sat herself beside Rose, squeezed her knee gently, and asked her what had happened.

"I was walking to you from my house when a chunky black car

sped past me ever so fast, and I had to jump into the hedge to get out of its path before they mowed me down!"

"Do you think you should report it? Did you get the number plate? Are you hurt, sweetie?" came the onslaught of questions from Val.

Rose replied, "I would love to report it, but I don't know the number of the car, just that it was a dark grey or black colour and there was a silver logo on the back of the car just above the number plate. It was very shiny and possibly very new. I am not hurt, just shaken up a bit. They were probably running late for work or something. I do wish people would slow down. It's a good job I was not riding a bike or, worse, a horse. A horse would have been spooked for sure with a car speeding past so fast. They didn't see me in the daylight, can you imagine what would have happened if it was dark, or dusk as well? There is no excuse for driving like that, none at all." Rose sipped her tea and grimaced at the sweetness of the tea, "How many sugars did you put in this, Val?"

"I lost count, just a couple and a few more, I think. You sure you're OK? Did you hit your head?"

"Positive, I am just pleased I was on my way to your place and not on my way home as I do feel a bit shaky and out of sorts, you know?"

Val jumped up to get her scones out of the oven for her new guests and handed a plate to Rose with a freshly baked hot scone which was liberally buttered. The butter was dripping over the sides of the scone and smelt divine.

Rose munched the scone and contemplated the events of the last few days and those of the last few months since Christmas and then shared her concerns with Val. Val agreed that it was all a bit odd and concerning but she encouraged Rose to focus on her open day and offered to bake some cakes, biscuits, and scones to welcome her potential customers. They talked over how to get the best out of the day and that Rose could give a short presentation using the skills she already had from her previous job, if she wanted to. Rose talked about her relationship with Tom and was reassured that Val agreed with her that she just needed to have a chat with him. Val's sensible motherly advice was to talk it out and tell him how she felt about him and the future. The afternoon whizzed by, the incident on the way almost forgotten, until she got up to walk back home down the lane. It was getting dark by then, Val's guests were late, so David offered to run her home back up the lane in the car.

David was happy to take her home and often run her back in the car if she stayed late or needed him to. He was a lovely guy and Rose hoped that one day there would be someone like that for her, always at her side to help her and her friends if they needed him. When she hopped out of his car and waved goodbye to David from her front door, she knew she needed to have a serious chat with Tom. As David drove away, after getting her to wave goodbye so that he knew that all was well with her, she realised that she wanted and needed a guy just like that.

She wouldn't have long to wait as she was seeing Tom the following day. They had planned to explore the folly together on the way to the beach. A winter walk followed by a long cosy afternoon by the fire and maybe a takeaway or something tasty for dinner. Tom hadn't asked to stay over, but she wasn't expecting him to leave until late on Sunday night or even Monday morning. She was looking forward to seeing him but didn't really want to have 'that chat'. Things were good with Tom, nothing a few little tweaks and a little reassurance from him wouldn't sort. She hated to be clingy or needy, she just wanted to know what was going on with him and where he saw things going. She was still mulling everything around in her head as she lay in bed that night with Mowzer asleep next to her, curled into her stomach for warmth. As she lay in the darkness, the silence was broken by the noise of a car being driven fast along the lane beside the house. Another speeding car, sounding just like the one that nearly hit her. It sped past and the sound faded into the distance. She dozed in the silence that followed until she was awoken again by the sound of the same car driving slower, much slower, coming to a halt just outside the house. She crept out of bed slowly, moving the curtain very slightly so she couldn't be seen, and looked out. There was a car, a big dark car, stationary outside.

It stayed for a minute or two, looking in, and then slowly drove off back along the lane.

## Twenty-Seven

Rose was ready for Tom when he arrived on Saturday morning, she had her sturdy walking boots on and was wrapped up well against the weather. It was still bitterly cold, the recent warm spell just a flash in the pan. Rose had started to hunt out some t-shirts and lightweight clothing when it had turned warm, but typically the British weather had a way of flummoxing her plans. She was wearing a brightly coloured hat with a huge pom-pom on the top, which she loved but Tom reckoned made her look ridiculous. She was pottering about outside, checking the outbuildings and making sure the outside taps were still well lagged against the cold when his van pulled up.

"It is like going out with someone with two heads when you wear that silly hat, Rose," he teased as he got out of the van. He was wearing a dark quilted jacket that Rose had never seen before.

She retorted, "At least you won't lose me on the walk this morning. If you step in any shadows, I won't see you at all."

"I am doing very well out of my new winter job, so I treated myself to a new jacket. Don't be rude, Rose, or I won't treat you with my extra cash later. A little internet shopping when we get back. Shucks, nothing for Rose ... ahh!"

A swift gentle punch to the arm was all the response he got from Rose and a childish giggle.

"A new job, Tom? You never told me! Tell me all about it on the way. I want all the details."

"Not much to tell but it has kept me busier than expected during the last few weeks and I know I have been very preoccupied. But then so have you, so we definitely need to catch up."

He slung his arm around Rose, and they crossed the yard together toward the footpath. "Be nice to have a chat with you without the boys on the job. Nice that you have got the place back to yourself for a bit. Perhaps I can get you all to myself again too!"

As they walked on in companionable silence, Rose chewed over the last few words, it *had* been a bit maniac in the house and in the adjoining outbuildings while everyone had been pitching in with all the work. Mickey had almost taken up permanent residence in the utility room in the afternoons, enjoying all the company with Bert at his feet. She had not noticed that she hadn't had much 'alone' time with Tom. He had been popping in on his way home from work, staying for a short while and going straight back to his flat as he was shattered. She had seen him every day, but not really seen him at all. She also pondered on his choice of words, going over the conversation in her head, as all women are inclined to do, dissecting every word for a hidden meaning. The telling phrase was 'I have been very preoccupied lately'. She concluded that Val had rang him yesterday after she had left to tell him about the incident on the way to hers and to prewarn him about her impending 'chat' with him. There was only one way to find out, she wasn't going to ask him as that was too easy. She was going to be sneaky.

"I didn't sleep too well last night, Tom," she said, breaking the silence and snuggling in closer to his chest as they strolled along together.

"Well, that was because I wasn't with you," he replied, winking knowingly at her. "It must have been very cold and very lonely without me."

She wanted to smile, grin, or give a cheeky response but she stayed silent and slowly counted to five, she only got to three before he interjected, "It might have been because of that near miss on the way to Val's. You sure you are, OK?"

She could not stop her giggle then, it escaped with a rush of air, making her raise her gloved hand to her face to try to stop more giggles escaping. Tom looked down at her at his side and gave her a shove.

"OK, that was so sneaky, you had me there. Yeah, I have had a chat with Val who told me how you felt about things and what happened to you yesterday. How did you guess? I was being so careful. You …" His words drifted off in frustration as he knew he had been firmly caught out.

With a big meaningful sigh, he drew her close to him again and leaned down to kiss her, kissing her cheek first and then deftly catching her chin and turning her face to his. He kissed her affectionately and firmly on the lips. Reaching up she wound her hands around his neck and drew him to her, returning his kiss and turning it into a passionate embrace. Each of them was so lost in the moment they did not see the figure behind them dart back into the trees that lined the footpath.

## Twenty-Eight

As they got closer to the folly, they got closer again as a couple. They reluctantly continued their walk when every fibre of their being was telling them to head back to the house, snuggle up and reignite their passion in bed. As they were walking, they weren't thinking of which romantic film to watch or which novel to read when they got back, but both of them were thinking about making romantic moves of their own. They were still walking closely together when the footpath's width would allow it but if it didn't they resembled a demented crab walking sideways if they had to, as they were so unwilling to take their hands of each other.

Tom thought he had dodged a bullet when he got the hint from Val that Rose was upset with him again. He knew he had been a bit odd lately, but when his working life had taken a bit of an unexpected turn, he couldn't get used to his new routine and until he had got it all sorted, he was unsure of burdening Rose with it too. The only advantage, it seemed, was the extra cash, which was very welcome for a gardener in the winter months. He was going to wait until they got back to the house before he discussed it with Rose properly.

Rose was just pleased that she had her 'old' Tom back. He was a man of few words most of the time, but she knew he cared and was positive that he loved her as much as she loved him. When she got closer to the folly, she pulled away from Tom and stuck her hands in her pockets, searching for the bunch of keys that Tom had found on

Christmas morning when he had reached out of the window searching for the ornament from the Christmas tree. The folly had been locked up for years. No one had known where the keys were and even though the building was on her land, she had never explored the inside She had just accepted the keys were lost and had never made any attempts to find them. She had been too busy with the house ever since she had moved in.

The door was solid, and the lock was too. Rock solid. She had tried to nudge it open like the cops on the telly with her shoulder and a swift kick on a previous visit, but it wouldn't budge a whisker without a key. The door contained two large iron hinges and a large iron lock, but she now had a large iron key with two smaller keys in her pocket. She had already tried the keys in some of the outbuildings and randomly around the house. The keys were oddly shaped and fitted nothing so far. She was hoping the big key would fit the door of the folly. If it didn't, she was going to ask Tom to do the big shoulder nudge and kick as it always worked on the telly. If all else failed, she was going to ask Phyliss in the antique shop if she had any more keys lying around that she could try. Where would you find a locksmith that dealt with very old doors? She didn't know but she was sure that Phyliss would.

She edged into the undergrowth along the foot of the tower, making her way to the door. She did not care about her jacket as it was already ripped from the events of the day before. The undergrowth was worn down and the branches were broken in several parts where someone had made another path in. It was clear that someone else had been trying to get into the folly. There were several new marks to the door and the lock had a long scrape along one side.

Tom followed her path and took in the damage to the shrubs, trees, and door as she did. They shared an anxious look. Without trying the key in the lock, they continued to follow the trampled undergrowth around the base of the tower and came out the way they came in. Rose walked around the back of the bench and looked for any other signs of interference. There were none. Tom checked for more sinister activity, looking for the glint of light on the surface of a camera or binoculars or the buzz of a low-flying drone.

The figure following had already stepped behind an old oak tree and could not be seen. They were still watching.

A solitary crow flew along the footpath, followed by another and another. Then the sky was full of crows, flying together before coming to roost on the top of the tower, like a flock of sentries keeping a watchful eye on the couple below and the figure hidden from sight. The crows turned their heads as one and fixed their beady stares at the old oak. They knew the stranger was there. Tom and Rose were however completely unaware that they were being watched.

The crows remained perched on the tower, silently watching, as Rose and Tom disappeared into the undergrowth at the base of the tower. Rose held the keys in her hand and slid the larger key on the iron ring into her fingers and tried the key in the lock.

The key slid into the orifice of the lock and seemed to fit well. Rose looked at Tom.

"Just get on with it will you, stop being such a drama queen. Get you, pausing for dramatic effect. Does it open the damn door?" Tom teased.

With a slight tug and a bit of a wiggle the key turned in the lock, almost all the way, but it was now firmly stuck. Rose could not turn it either left or right or even take the key out of the lock.

"Let me have a go. You just need to be firm." Tom gently held her shoulders before she could get cross and make it worse. He grabbed the key and wiggled it too. It was still stuck firm but the air surrounding them changed, producing peculiar smells, a whiff of incense, perfume, and then tobacco smoke. Then smoke whirled around them, creating a grey mist that completely surrounded them both. A wisp of the mist flowed gently downwards towards the door and the key. The mist flowed onto the key and through the keyhole and beyond. Rose and Tom were mesmerised by the mist and followed it intently with their eyes as it vanished through the keyhole. The tobacco smell lingered, the same tobacco scent from the house that Rose was so familiar with. The perfume that was mixed in was exotic but also vaguely familiar to Rose. She put her fingers on Tom's and they tried again together. This time, the key turned the whole way, and the door was unlocked but still firmly stuck. With a grin, Tom turned to Rose and put his shoulder to the door. The door opened with an almighty bang as it hit the stone of the wall behind it. It was just shut, not stuck at all. Rose caught Tom before he landed squarely on his face on the floor. They then turned and stared.

## Twenty-Nine

They expected the tower to be empty inside with just stone walls and a cobbled or flagstone floor, but there was a wooden bench alongside one wall and stone staircase that led up. Rose thought that the building was just an empty shell which is why she had been so disinterested in it when she first inherited the house. When she had talked it over with Mickey after Christmas, he had said there must have been a staircase inside so that you could get to the top. It was an ideal look out and was surely built with that in mind. She thought that any wooden staircase would be totally unsafe by now, as the tower had looked incomplete from the outside and surely not watertight. It was a shock that it smelled musty, not damp, and there was a stone staircase, not a decaying set of stairs made of wood leading upwards.

"I am just as surprised as you, Rose. I can see by your face you expected it to be damp, green, and horrible in here. I expected to be knee deep in bird poo. What are you doing peering underneath the bench, you know you can't find priceless treasure everywhere you look? You were lucky with those paintings."

Bumping her head on the underside of the bench as she rose, she replied, "I wasn't looking for treasure, but I was looking for a carving on the wood. Give us a hand to turn it over, will you?"

Tom and Rose turned the bench over, Rose handed her woolly gloves to Tom and searched with her fingertips for any carvings, or

THE CAPTAIN'S FOLLY

anything scratched on the surface. The light was dim as there was only one small window high above them. Tom switched on his torch on his phone and directed it onto the bench.

"There looks like there is something right here. Very odd, just a weird pattern. No arrow," Rose exclaimed, looking intently at the roughly hewn scratches in the wood.

"No arrow? Girl, are you losing the plot? Are you on some sort of treasure hunt you are only telling me about now? Rose?" Tom was teasing, but Rose sensed his hurt that she had not shared a secret of her house with him. "Something to do with your captain, is it?"

Rose grinned, so pleased with herself that there was a sign that the captain was here, and it was his folly. She took a photo with her phone, messing about with the focus function to zoom right into the detail. Together they carefully placed the bench back in the same position and Rose took lots more photos. The camera's automatic flash coming on with every shot. It was eerier than she expected, and she was pleased she had Tom with her.

Tom meanwhile had gone back to the door and taken the key out of the lock and put it in his pocket. "I wouldn't fancy being shut up in here, even with you, for a second. Spooky. Not feeling the love from your captain right now. Are you, Rose?"

The circular stone staircase took up most of the room in the tower, spiralling anti-clockwise to the top. Spooky or not, Rose wanted to see more and was now standing on the bottom step waiting for Tom to join her. She wouldn't have thought about the key in the lock as she just wanted to explore and was desperate to see the view from the top. Reassured that he was right behind her, she slowly made her way up the stairs. She stopped to look out of the first window she came too. No glass, just an iron framework keeping the birds out which was why there were no bird droppings in the tower. The iron looked like a fairly recent addition. The view was spectacular, even from the lowest window, and she could see back across the footpath to her house and outbuildings. She wasn't looking for anything specific but couldn't miss the oak tree laden with crows. It appeared to be black blossom or fruit from a distance until they all took flight in unison. One mass of flapping black wings, all blending into one. A flock of crows taking to the skies at once. It was then that she saw the figure looking back at her from the base of the trees, completely unaware of the crows that had just taken flight. The figure stood, stared intently at the folly, then vanished behind the tree from whence he came. Tom was perched on the same step, albeit on the narrow bit of the stone stair. He saw the crows take to the skies, but not the figure.

"I don't like this place, Rose. Did you know that the old English collective term for a group of crows is a 'murder' of crows? So sinister, don't you think? Also, did you know that crows are omnivorous scavengers? They eat carrion, you know. Appearing on battlefields to pick at the remains of the dead. The death birds. Eergh!"

"You are such a cheerful chappie today, aren't you, Tom? Did you see that man? Do you think he is following us? Did you take the key out of the lock because you saw him?" she said.

"Of course I didn't see him' otherwise I would have waited and confronted him. I just thought what with the business about your card in the window and that black car that almost run you down yesterday we needed to be careful. This was also the place that Mickey had his accident and we never got to the bottom of what happened to him, did we? He says he can't remember, doesn't he? Have you noticed he has not been up here since and this was always part of his daily walk with Bert? He loved sitting on that bench watching everything around him. Bert still wants to come up here, I have seen Mickey tugging the lead pulling Bert to either your place or up the lane to Val's. Mickey never turns up the footpath anymore. Very odd."

They both stood at the window watching for the man to move again to see which way he had gone. Tom was holding onto Rose's shoulders for his support as much as hers. Rose was fearless as she suspected that the figure was her captain. She felt none of the uneasiness that Tom did, no ambivalence to the figure. Tom's mouth was next to her ear, but it was not his voice or his words that whispered into it, "Beware."

# *Thirty*

Rose turned her head to look at Tom and she stared into a pair of blue eyes that were as familiar to her as her own, but they were not Tom's. His features were worn and ruddy and his hair was a different shade. His eyes were stern and full of warning and Rose wanted to look away. She couldn't, she was compelled to return the stare and look into his eyes, searching for more. She felt a cold chill and shivered. His eyes were a piercing blue, he sensed her chill and felt her fear. From the dullness of the stairwell, barely visible, his eyes changed from stern to love with a glimmer of humour. His eyes focused just beyond her, so she turned to follow his gaze.

"What are you warning me about? Please tell me more. Please," she begged.

As she turned back, he kissed her gently, so gently. Looking up, it was Tom's eyes on hers once again. Full of reassurance and love, she kissed Tom back, all the while wondering whether she had kissed her captain or Tom moments before.

Tom gave Rose a gentle shove to get her moving again. He wanted to find out what was at the top. He didn't want Rose to linger watching crows, figures, or anything else from the window. He needed to get going, see what the folly was all about and get back to the house. He wanted to protect her first and foremost and hated the pair of them being vulnerable. He planned to walk her home swiftly past the old oak tree, as he reckoned whoever it was would be long gone and he was going to investigate on his own later, once Rose was safe and sound indoors. To his dismay, Rose was feeling all amorous and kissy. Not what he wanted in the middle of a stone staircase, he wanted to get going. Get moving.

Both of them followed the spiral staircase to the top. Almost at the top, Tom squeezed past her to be first. The staircase ended abruptly but they saw that a wooden floor had been laid alongside the staircase and there were small holes in the tower to look out from. There was some kind of hatch in the roof covering. It was all watertight, but Tom tested his weight on some of the boards before walking out onto it just to be sure. The wood creaked and the whole structure seemed to sigh as the creaking was amplified within the empty shell.

"Tempting as this is, Rose, my love. I think we should come back another day with Steve or one of his builder friends, or even that conservation guy from the council. Judging by the amount of dust and dirt, no one has been up here for years. It could be unsafe."

Grabbing her arm, he pulled her away from the edge of the stone spiral and coaxed her down the stairs.

"Not the time to be looking for any more carvings and other signs from your captain. I am cold, hungry, and tired enough for a long, cosy afternoon nap," he winked at Rose.

Rose could still hear the Captain's 'beware' resonating in her head. She was still picturing his dear face and had not really regained her equilibrium at all from earlier. To Tom's surprise, she needed no further persuading to be coaxed down the stairs. She did not linger by the window, but without slowing his pace and letting on to Rose, Tom peered out, checking that the figure had gone. There was no one to be seen, apart from a pair of crows lazily circling in a thermal high up in the sky, still watching over the folly. Silently keeping their beady eyes on everything below.

As Tom locked the door behind them, Rose took more photos of the folly from the ground, focusing the camera on her phone as much as she could on the top of the tower. The roof could not be seen from the ground, indeed the tower looked like the ruin, they had expected it to be knee deep in bird droppings when they stepped inside. It was very exciting. She wished she had brought a bigger camera with a better zoom or even had a drone to play with.

Tom sat down on the bench while Rose was taking the photos and exploring the base of the tower. He looked across at the thicket of trees, dominated by the old oak. No crows could be seen perching on the tree, and he could see no signs of other life. The bench was a good place to sit and think. Tom couldn't understand why Mickey would not come back to his regular haunt. He resolved to ask him the next time he saw him. Or better still, he might invite himself onto Mickey's regular walk with Bert and turn him back along the footpath. His thoughts turned to drone footage, there might already be some footage on the internet. He would have to do some digging.

They both headed back to the house along the footpath. Tom stopped to look back at the folly when they came to the thicket of trees on the way back, to distract Rose from looking too intently for signs of the mysterious figure. Rose stopped when he did.

The crows were lined up on the roof once more, like a line of sentries on guard.

As Rose and Tom turned back to the house, the faint outline of two more figures appeared on the bench. The figures became clearer and more distinct, and a plume of tobacco smoke rose into the cold air from the pipe that the Captain held in his hands. His companion did not keep watch as he did, she gazed up adoringly into the face of the man she loved. Happy to be at his side once more.

The captain continued to keep watch over his house, his folly, and his land. He would always watch but would not always be visible.

When she turned and looked back at the folly, the couple had vanished, replaced on the bench by a couple of magpies, which had landed on the wooden slats of the bench at the moment they disappeared. Not before she had caught a faint glimpse of the Captain and his lady beside him. Just a hint. She raised her fingers to her lips, remembering the kiss, and smiled wistfully as he faded away, leaving just a trace of tobacco smoke in his wake.

## Thirty-One

Tom popped back up to the folly on his own some days later and didn't find any evidence of anything untoward by the old oak tree that looked across at the folly. There were footprints around the base of the tree but nothing to suggest anything suspicious. The tall trees were full of crows' nests and were often to be seen on the folly building itself. The oak tree was growing alongside a footpath with several others, and a small path led off the main footpath towards the thicket. Dense ivy crept up the trees, carpeting them in a shroud of green. There were smaller paths through the thicket that were obviously used by dogs, foxes, and other animals. Tom spotted some rabbit droppings, what looked like an owl pellet, and a small pile of very smelly fox poo. Nothing more.

He wasn't really expecting to find anything, but he wanted to make sure. He also needed to see how much of a vantage point the tree was. There was a clear view of the folly, the house, and the outbuildings from the tree. It was a big tree but not an easy one to climb and there were no signs that anyone had attempted to climb the tree. However, in the summer when the tree had its leaves, being amongst its branches would be an excellent hiding place, hidden from those on the ground. His actions were not going unnoticed by a pair of magpies that perched silently in the oak tree above him, watching his every move with their black beady eyes.

Tom had not managed to find the right time to discuss the folly with Mickey. Mickey was still avoiding it and the footpath, but Tom wasn't sure whether it was the lure of his Auntie Val's baking that was sending him in that direction. Mickey still popped in to see Rose on the way to Val's, craftily managing to have two cuppas and two slices of cake on most of his walks. He knew Rose was secretly pleased that he was not going to the folly as she worried about him. Rose wouldn't stop worrying until they knew what had happened up there when Mickey had his fall.

Thankfully, Mickey was now fully recovered although he still claimed that he could not remember anything of that day, apart from seeing Rose and ending up in the hospital. Tom thought it was only a matter of time before Mickey remembered or he was willing to tell them.

Rose had hidden the key to the folly somewhere unbeknown to even Tom. It was the only part of her inheritance that she was unsure about, and the constant whispered warnings and spooky bell ringing had prompted her to file it in the 'too difficult' part of her brain, parking it for a while. She was glad she took Tom with her when she managed to unlock the folly and get inside. It was a spooky, empty place, the complete opposite of the first time she visited her house. The house was reputed to be haunted, very forlorn, and extremely dishevelled but she had loved the house from when she first set eyes on it. When she ventured inside the house for the first time, it seemed to envelop her in a big hug. It was warm, welcoming, and 'home'. Whenever she thought of the folly, she kept seeing Trevor fleeing from the tower, scared witless, or Mickey on a stretcher being carried to the waiting ambulance. The backdrop of the imposing tower of the folly constantly in her mind's eye.

It contrasted completely with the delicate, loving kiss on the steps of the tower. The kiss that happened after that whisper of 'beware'.

Was the Captain warning her about the folly or the figure that she spotted from the window? The crows seemed to roost and call the folly their home. Little sentries beadily watching all below from the tower. Friendly or dangerous? Rose couldn't make it out. The folly door was now firmly locked again on the tower and Rose was going to keep it that way until she could work out what to do with it, or if she should just let the crows live in peace and leave well alone, as it seemed everyone had done for years. She ignored the irrational part of her brain that kept remembering the kiss. That kiss. That passion. She still continued to wonder if that was her Tom or her captain.

She had enough on her plate getting her head around Tom's new job. He was still working for himself, but he had been manoeuvred into working for just the one couple for a couple of months. Reworking the old garden of an old manor house. The couple had recently moved into a new property on the site of an old manor house which had been demolished back in the sixties and replaced by a little bungalow. This bungalow had been recently knocked down by the couple and a modern sprawling mansion had been built in its place. It was tall and imposing with lots of open-plan living space. The house had huge glass windows and most of the exterior walls were made of toughened glass. Tom told Rose it would be like living in a fish tank, glass on all sides. The couple that had built the house stated that it 'brought the outside in'. So, it was now Tom's job, in their words, to 'snazzy up' the outside to match. They wanted the old flower beds to be updated and filled with modern varieties of the old roses. This was the real reason Tom had wanted the job, because they wanted to get rid of all the old shrub roses as they weren't in keeping with their plans. Tom wanted those plants and quoted for the job, not for the new planting but so that he could go home with the old planting and the old varieties of the roses that he loved.

Tom told her that the couple were demanding, and the job was a big job to a small timescale. They wanted to show off the garden in the spring and early summer to their friends, with instant results. They were extremely hard to work for in the short daylight hours that was all he had to work with in the winter months, which had meant that Rose was not given top priority. He was shattered as he was dropping the old plants to Sam at the nursery on his way to his flat or Rose's when he finished work for the day. His daily commute was insane, but once the big job was finished, he would have plenty of roses and other traditional planting to grow on, study, and cherish. He had big plans with the money he was earning from this job. It seemed that the pair of them, Tom and Rose, had big plans and very little time and energy for each other.

Like Tom's new clients really. He had only met the wife, Judith, who was lovely. He had never met her husband, who was always away working hard he was told. Judith's husband was the one with the big ideas and used his 'big' money to pay for them.

By the end of the weekend when they had explored the folly, Rose and Tom had agreed to make more time for each other. Tom only had a few weeks left of his schedule to finish the job. The couple were keen to take him on a permanent basis as a regular gardener, but their house was just a little too far away for it to be a feasible business decision for Tom. There was also talk of them moving on to something new when the garden was finished and there was nothing left to do. Tom found their constant thirst for the latest trend and designs exhausting. He would be happy to leave them to it and never see the garden again! He often wondered how he came to tender for the job in the first place. They had called him, but never said how they knew of him or who recommended him. He just knew he wasn't really given the opportunity to turn them down or refuse to work for them. He often wondered, why are there people like that in life, who always seem to get their own way?

## Thirty-Two

Rose stood on the footpath by the oak tree and looked up at the folly. She was not sure why she had wandered up this way. It was early in the morning, and she had not eaten her breakfast or had her regular morning cuppa in bed. This particular morning, she had wanted to get up and about. She normally pottered about the house for a bit, after having a leisurely cup of tea in bed. She enjoyed her new lazy morning routine which was the complete opposite of the way her mornings used to be when she lived and worked in London. Then, she was up at 'silly o'clock', crammed on the heaving transport system commuting to work with everyone else. Desperately trying to respect everyone's personal space but being unable to avoid getting squashed into someone's back, side, or, the worse possible scenario, their smelly, sweaty armpit! She had the key to the folly in her pocket and needed to have another poke around up there on her own. Well, that's what she thought she wanted to do until she got to the oak tree and remembered the sinister figure that she saw from the folly with Tom. She started to change her mind, changing her direction of travel as she did so.

She came to a halt at the end of the footpath, where it came out into the lane alongside her outbuildings. She had nearly walked out into the lane without looking out for the traffic. Surely she would have heard a car coming along the lane, but she berated herself for her inattention just the same. Particularly stupid as she had almost been knocked in the air a couple of weeks ago by a speeding black car. Instead, she almost got knocked into the air this morning by Mickey, who was walking along the lane with Bert and just a few seconds later she would have either tripped over Bert or crashed into Mickey.

Mickey was surprised and very bemused to see Rose up and about so early.

He greeted her with a cheery smile, "Hello you, what are you doing up at this time, did you wet the bed?"

Rose grinned back at him, "No, I didn't, cheeky! I just wanted to get out and about, get some fresh air and start the day. I have the key to the folly in my pocket, I was going to go up there and have a poke about again."

Mickey looked at Rose and raised his eyebrows as well as his arms. "Why were you rushing out into the lane then, the folly is up the footpath, up that way there?"

"Well, I got spooked by the oak tree in the thicket on the way. Weird, I know. Would you come along with me, keep me company with Bert? He looks like he wants to go that way. The two of us can't get up to too much mischief, can we? We will have Bert to look after us. What do you say, come with me? Have a look inside the folly?"

She tugged his arm gently and then reached down to stroke Bert. She crouched down to Bert's level and fondled his ears. She loved Bert's big floppy Spaniel ears best of all. Soft, silky, and a lovely nut-brown colour. Bert loved a cuddle with Rose and clambered up onto her knees, trying to sit on her lap, even as she was just crouching down and there wasn't a lap for him to sit on. Bert managed to give her big sloppy Spaniel kisses all over her face while she was within reach and while Mickey was making up his mind which way to go.

Mickey was torn, he looked up the footpath and back at Rose. He didn't say a word. Rose watched his face and saw all manner of emotions in his eyes and facial expressions. From scared to frightened, then longing. Eventually, Mickey's resolve and stubbornness took over. He was not going to let the place get the better of him. He took Rose's hand as she reached out to him, drew her back up on her feet, and continued to hold her hand, with a nod. They walked together back up the footpath towards the folly, an eager Bert at their feet. Mickey reached down and released his lead from his harness and let Bert run free. Bert didn't need telling, he knew the way. He raced off, darting from side-to-side, sniffing anything interesting to his inquisitive Spaniel nose. Having a sniff at all the 'wee mails' that had been left by other animals. Bert reached the thicket first and they lost sight of him. They could hear him snuffling with delight in the undergrowth, having his own little adventures.

"This is the first time we have come this way since you found me on the ground by the folly that day. The first time my Bert has been off the lead since. He needs his space, bless him. I couldn't walk this way on my own, when he goes off. I don't like being on my own outside the house without Bert on his lead beside me. I am a silly old fool, Rose."

"Of course, you're not. You have just been sensible; I really don't blame you either. You had a bit of a shock that day, didn't you? Do you remember what happened? Do you want to talk about it?"

"I do remember some of what happened, but I am not sure of everything that did. Do you see what I mean? I was up there sitting on my bench with Bert doing his usual exploring stuff and I heard a noise. I don't know what the noise was, that's the bit I can't remember, silly old fool I am. I got up too quick I think, startled by the noise, and I remember I felt scared, really, really scared. All alone. I couldn't see Bert and, all of a sudden, I was on the ground. I couldn't move much, and my head hurt. I looked up and saw the crows flying. They went round and round in a circle above me. I heard voices, muttering. Muttering. I don't know what they said, that bit is still unclear. I was scared, so frightened, and so alone. Then there was a strange man peering over me and thankfully I saw you, Rose. You I remember, you were there with Bert. Looking after me. You looked scared too. Very scared of that man. Rose." Mickey started to ramble quietly under his breath, so his words were incomprehensible to her. Rose squeezed his hand to let him know she was still there.

"No need to tell me anymore, Mickey. Let's just walk together and enjoy the morning."

## *Thirty-Three*

They walked along together, holding hands. Both of them seeking support from each other. Rose had not mentioned the figure near the folly that she had seen with Tom a couple of weekends ago to Mickey. She didn't want to worry him. Unbeknown to her, Mickey was wrestling with secrets and memories of his own. They strolled hand in hand, side by side, only letting go of each other's hand when the footpath got narrow.

When they reached the base of the folly and the old tower loomed above them, Mickey gave an audible sigh and sat down on the bench. Bert jumped up beside him. Mickey smiled broadly and Bert did his best to mirror that smile with a doggy version of his own. Mickey and Bert looked around them and then back at Rose.

"Rose, my love, I can't tell you how much it means to me to be back here. I am so pleased that you cajoled me into coming back. This is my spot, well, my late wife, Iris, and mine – our place. Our special place. We often sat here together and watched the wildlife and the world go on around us. In the summer we would have a picnic up here and bring the dogs. We were never blessed with children. Our dogs were our children. In the winter we would still bring a picnic. A winter picnic, a flask of hot strong coffee and some freshly baked cake. You know how much I love my cake, Rose," he chortled.

"I know how much you like your cake; I am sure you pop into mine and Val's most days just to eat our cake. It's got nothing at all to do with us, has it?"

"I have been rumbled, my love. You need to bake more; I prefer a home-cooked cake to those ones you buy in the local shop with your newspaper. I will lend you Iris's recipe book. She cut out recipes from magazines and newspapers when she saw one she liked. It's more like a scrapbook really. I know you will take good care of it. Just keep it to yourself, don't share. It has the recipe that she used to win first prize in the cake competition most years at the local fete. She would have loved to have passed it down to her children, but we never had any. Not for the want of trying. We shed tears together up here when we realised we were going to remain childless. We considered fostering, but she wanted her own. Her own little girls to pass on all her wisdom, advice, and recipes to. She would have loved you, as I do. I've not known you long, but you are the daughter we both wished for. Come here, my love. Let me give you a big hug. Off you get Bert. Let Rose have the seat."

He gave Bert a shove and shuffled over for Rose to sit by the side of him. Rose shyly sat down and was enveloped in a big hug, with Mickey's arm squeezing her tightly. Mickey mopped his eyes with his other hand, wiping the tears that had welled during his unexpected, emotional speech. Then he buried his head in Rose's coat and shed more tears onto her shoulder.

Rose was surprised by this unexpected display of emotion. She knew they had become firm friends, but when he called her the daughter they never had, she was taken aback by the depth of the friendship that they had formed. She knew how lucky she was to have gained Mickey's respect so quickly. Mickey could be a prickly old man if he didn't like you or you upset him. There was no rhyme or reason why sometimes. He harboured grudges towards others in the village that had been going on so long, no one quite remembered what it was all about when she asked. To be given his wife's recipe scrapbook, even to borrow for a short time, was a real privilege.

"If you let me borrow that scrapbook, you know I will have no excuse not to bake you a 'proper' cake. Are you prepared for the consequences of your actions?" she retorted.

"Oh, I am sure I will eat whatever you bake. May I suggest you start with what my wife tactfully referred to as her 'throw in' fruit cake. You just measure all the ingredients into a bowl, give it a quick stir, and then chuck it into a cake tin and bake it in the oven. She reckoned even I could do it! Perhaps I could have a go too. You and I could have a 'bake off' like that show on the telly. What do you think?"

With a giggle, Rose replied, "I don't think she ever just chucked it into a cake tin. Seriously, Mickey! You and me in a 'bake off' sounds fun. I know, to shake it up even more, I could come over to you for tea and cake, as you always come to me."

"Loving the idea, Rose. I could get the best china tea set out and host a little tea party. We could invite Val to be the judge of the cakes. I will drop the scrapbook over to you tomorrow. Not sure her secret recipe of her 'throw in' fruit cake will be in her scrapbook, will have a hunt about in the cottage for it. She might have popped it in her safe place." He nudged his nose with his index finger when he mentioned the secret place.

All thoughts of going into the folly were forgotten, with all the talk of his wife, longed-for children, and the all-important soon-to-be bake off between the pair of them. When they started to get cold, they sauntered back the way they came. Closer than ever, an unlikely trio, but looking to all intents and purposes a family. Rose's new friends were becoming her 'family' and those, she reckoned, were the very best friends to have.

It was very prudent that they never tried to unlock the folly as there was someone hidden from sight listening to every word. Almost concealed in the undergrowth and the unruly ivy that crept up unhindered on the walls. He was silent and still, until they walked away far enough for him not to be spotted. Then he made his way back to the door of the folly and tried the latch again. The door refused to budge as the iron key was missing from the lock. The key that was nestled in Rose's coat pocket as she strode away.

## Thirty-Four

That evening, when Rose went to bed, the black car had already parked up tucked out of sight in the gateway of a field a short way from the house. The occupant of the car darted behind the fence post at the entrance to her driveway when Rose was seen in the window, drawing the curtains and having a last look out of the window before getting into bed.

She had popped into the local supermarket that afternoon to stock up on baking ingredients and to buy a cake tin. She popped a couple of cookery magazines into her trolley and a 'how to bake a cake' book which was currently in the bestsellers top 10. She hopped into bed and pushed Mowzer to the bottom so she could spread her new magazines and book next to her. She had already looked everything up using the internet function on her phone, but as an old-fashioned girl at heart, she still was doing a bit more research on paper.

Rose was engrossed in all things baking and didn't hear the footsteps crunching on the gravel as the intruder crept up the drive. She didn't hear the rattle of the door handle at the front and back door as they tried both handles to gain access to the house. Mowzer did, he jumped off the bed unbeknown to Rose and pattered down the stairs, leaping on the kitchen work surface to watch the figure turn the corner towards the other buildings in the yard.

All of a sudden Mowzer was on the other side of the window. He was not alone. He trotted alongside his companion, looking up trustily into his master's face. More like a little dog than a cat. Showing no fear, they both rounded the corner and stood quietly in the shadows, watching the intruder try to get into every single one of the buildings before peering into the windows with a torchlight. Then, turning back, they shone the light into the shadows where Mowzer was concealed. Mowzer sat very still and let the torchlight reflect off his eyes. He stared, unblinking at the intruder and then up at his master for reassurance. His master was in the shadows, but the glow of his pipe could be seen, illuminating a section of his slightly greying black beard. He exhaled through the pipe and the wisps of smoke curled around his face, showing his eyes with his cool unflinching, piercing stare. His captain's hat cast extra shadows on his lined face. Mowzer and the Captain caught the imposter, like a rabbit in the headlights, in their stares.

The captain raised his hand and clenched his fist. Then he vanished from Mowzer's side, reappearing across the yard, his fist making a shadow across the face of the imposter. The captain's eyes just inches from theirs. The smoke whirled around the pair and then they were gone. Both of them, the Captain and the intruder.

As the smoke whirled, Mowzer found himself back behind the glass and could only look out of the window for his master that was no longer there. He knocked on the glass with his paw, frantic to join his master again, anxious for his wellbeing. He walked up and down the windowsill until he wore himself out and then stretched out to sleep on the sill.

Rose saw Mowzer there in the early hours when she came downstairs for a glass of water. She had not taken a glass to bed with her as she had her hands full of magazines and books the evening before. He had fallen asleep with his nose pressed to the glass and his bottom wedged between the taps of the sink. She was surprised he was even asleep as he looked so uncomfortable. When she turned on the tap to fill her glass, he didn't stir. She left him sleeping and crept back up the stairs to bed.

As the dawn broke, the occupant of the black car was woken from his deep slumber. His hands rubbed his eyes as he tried hard to remember the events of the night before. He remembered looking into angry eyes, feeling threatened. He shivered in his wet clothes, the smell of the sea permeated the air and the wisp of tobacco lingered.

Mowzer woke as the light grew and he crept into the still wet captain's hat that was now sitting beside him on the sill. He sniffed the hat intently then curled up tight and rested his chin on the brim. His eyes drooped contentedly as he drifted back to sleep.

## Thirty-Five

When Rose awoke it was quite late, she had slept soundly, and the events of the night had passed her by. She had slept like a log and her head pounded with the inevitable headache that she always got when she overslept. She stretched out in the bed and glanced over to the window trying to guess what kind of weather it was without getting up. She was cosy and warm and really didn't want to stir. She heard what sounded like heavy rain lashing the windowpane. She could hear the wind howling around the trees. Branches could be heard tapping on the dining room window below her. She decided that the better option was to stay in bed for a while as it sounded stormy and nasty outside.

She had lots to do to arrange her open day for her outbuildings. While she had been procrastinating, Tilly and Dotty had sorted out most of the arrangements for her between themselves. They had even set a date, to stop Rose from making any more excuses and just spending her time making lists and plans but not actually doing anything. Tilly had contacted most of the people on Dotty's list and a few extras she had thought of. Tilly reckoned that she needed a few wildcards, extra people that she knew but Rose didn't to liven it up a little. It was looking likely that it would be an 'invitation only' affair which would be easier to manage. Rose liked the idea of having people she liked working in her property. She had enough of office politics when she worked in the office in London. She liked Dotty and was wondering if she would be able to find the time to help her with some of the admin stuff. She was wasted in the local shop. Rose was going to have a good look at her finances to see if she could find the money to take her on in an admin capacity for a while to give her a hand with the start-up. However, it all depended on how well her venture went and how much money was left in the pot.

The weather raged outside as Rose dozed and contemplated her future. The magazines and book had fallen onto the floor in the night and lay discarded as Rose turned her thoughts to how long she would be able to keep going without some additional money coming in. She had retained some savings and there was some of her inheritance left as Steve was keeping the renovations to the house and outbuildings on budget. She still had the dining room at the front of the house to finish but hopefully that would be straight forward, and she could leave the one room till later on to completely finish. It was the only room that was not freshly plastered and was pretty much in its original state from when she looked at the house. Tom teased her that she was trying to leave what she perceived as the essence of the house intact and she would have to tackle that room one day. They had used the room at Christmas, using a lovely antique dining table and chairs that she had found under a sailcloth in one of the outbuildings with the other antique furniture. Rose's mum and dad had remarked that the room was very shabby chic, and shabby chic was bang on trend at the moment. Tom had used swathes of Christmas foliage to cover up the holes in the cornicing. A little Christmas tree in the grate instead of a fire worked a treat at Christmas. With the main lights off and just Christmas lights and candles, the 'oldy worldly' vibe worked wonders.

As she lay with her eyes shut, her mind wandering over anything and everything. She continued to listen to what was now clearly a storm raging outside. The wind had started to howl and there was an ominous creaking sound in the distance. The constant creaks and squeaks turned into what sounded like growls. Her sleepy mind pictured a wooden ship, creaking as it was tossed about on a raging, stormy sea. The growling a fierce sea monster of old, a sea dragon, a beast of the deep thrashing about in the waves alongside the ship.

Then there was a crash, a sickening thud with a high-pitched splintering sound. The ground and the house shook, the windows rattled, and the old house creaked in the storm. Then a loud boom. A single scream was heard before it was still, very still. The rain continued to fall steadily.

Rose couldn't shake the feeling that something was so very wrong, that something had happened. The scream was close, someone or something was in trouble. She got dressed in the clothes she had worn the day before and grabbed a hat from her dressing table to shove over her unbrushed hair. She raced downstairs, shoved her feet in her wellies, and put her raincoat on and ran out into the garden. Something had changed in the garden. At first, she didn't know what it was, until she got to the front gate and looked down the lane. A huge tree had been blown down and was blocking the road entirely. She could just make out a black shape underneath the tree. The beech tree had been growing in the far corner of the Captain's garden for centuries as it was so big. It had now taken a lump out of the garden as it was upended with its roots now clearly visible. There was a yawning gap in the hedge and an obstruction in the road. Rose was unconcerned about her garden or the road. What was the black shape under the tree itself?

## Thirty-Six

She took a detour back into her garden, walking around the tree's exposed roots and out the other side. The rain was coming down in stair rods, completely straight down, as the wind had dropped. The air was still. There was a menacing feeling in the air and Rose could still hear the single scream resonating in her head. As she came out of her garden back onto the lane, she saw David and Val running down the road towards her.

She waved to acknowledge them and to let them know that she was alright and turned her attention to the black shape that was hidden in the uppermost branches of the fallen tree. On closer inspection it was a black car, almost completely obliterated by the fallen tree. Squashed beyond recognition. Rose pulled the branches back to peer into the car to see if there was anyone inside and, if so, how badly they were hurt. The car appeared empty.

Val and David pulled branches aside and peered in as well when they arrived, keen to confirm, as Rose was, that there was nobody inside that needed immediate attention. The driving rain didn't help matters and everyone was wet through. Their clothes and waterproof coats plastered to their skin. Dripping, they continued to look into the branches and amongst the wreckage of the car to make certain there was nobody there.

They didn't notice someone appear from behind the trees bordering the fields. He looked white with shock and was staggering towards them, struggling to keep upright. He moaned as he walked, holding his head in his hands. His face contorted with the effort of staying on his feet.

Val and David heard the moan first as Rose was hidden amongst the branches with the car. They called out to Rose to help them and rushed to the man's side. Val gently encouraged him to sit down and searched for any visible injuries. There were none. He was shaken and didn't understand any questions but continued to moan. He was wet through too and any answers to Val's questions were incomprehensible. As Val pulled back the man's hood on his jacket and looked into his face, she recognised him immediately. The dazed man was Christian, who had stayed in the Captain's buildings in the winter months prior to Rose moving in. He hadn't been seen for many months, but was once a regular in the area, a homeless wanderer. He had made his home in one of the boats on the beach last summer and had vowed to make it seaworthy by the Spring. Living on the beach in the winter months would have been tough and no one was surprised when Christian went walkabout again.

"Christian, are you OK? Is this your car? What happened?" Val cried.

"I was walking along the lane last night and nipped into the field to watch the badgers that have a sett in the trees opposite your house. I was disturbed by a man parking in the entrance to the field. He blocked the gate, which really annoyed me, so I came by to take a note of his number plate. I was worried he might have heard about the badgers; people still bait badgers you know. By the time I had fired myself up to talk to him, as you know I don't like talking to strangers, he had walked off down the lane towards the Captain's House. I followed him at a distance, and he turned up your drive and I lost him then. I made my way back here and sat and waited for him to come back. He must have come back while I was dozing, I didn't hear him return but I heard him leave as he slammed the driver's door with such force, I am surprised you lot didn't hear him! Then he stomped off down the road back towards your place and the village. He was furious about something. Perhaps the car didn't start. Oh wow, he is going to be more than furious when he returns to find his car under that lot."

He sat shocked and swivelled to look at the remains of what looked like a very expensive black car, which was probably a complete write off underneath the trunk and branches of the mighty beech tree.

"Are you OK?" Rose cried when she saw Christian sitting on the floor looking up at Val and David as she emerged from the debris of the tree from her side of the lane. She ran towards him, brushing the foliage of the beech tree from her waterproof coat as she did so.

"What on earth happened to you? Why were you sleeping under the hedge here when you could have taken shelter in your usual building? I wondered where you were."

"Rose, I haven't been sleeping rough this year. Look at me, Rose. Do I look like I am still homeless? I have mended the rift between me and my dad and I am staying at his place up the coast for the winter. I plan to go back to the boat when the weather changes and spend the summer up there. I know you told me I would always be welcome with you, but you moving into the Captain's House prompted me to confront it all and sort it out. Thank you."

He got up on his feet and held his hands out to Rose. She took his hands in hers and then pulled him into a soggy embrace. Pleased that he was safe, and he not harmed.

"Trust you to be walking about checking on badgers. Really? How did you manage to sleep in this morning's storm?"

Christian looked at Rose, as did Val and David with puzzled expressions.

"It has been heavy rain since I got up this morning, Rose, but we have not had a storm. A slight wind maybe, but nothing to take down what looks like a healthy tree to me!" Val looked at Rose incredulously with a worried frown.

Rose was worried too. It was her tree that was across the road, and it wasn't a small job to get the road cleared for traffic. All her trees were surveyed before she bought the property, especially the larger ones. None of them were diseased and they were all deemed healthy. No one else heard the storm, the howling wind … Just her. Who and where was the owner of the car?

## *Thirty-Seven*

It didn't take long before a crowd of curious locals appeared on the village side of the fallen tree. Rose was always amazed how news travelled so fast in a village and how much the village folk seemed to know about their neighbours and the surrounding countryside. Last year, when most of the village had been flooded due to a wild summer storm, her house had remained untouched despite it being next to the river. The flood waters had formed a little moat around her house, leaving the house on its own little island. The flood water not causing any damage to the house, as if something or someone was keeping her and the house safe from harm.

There was a similar set of circumstances this time. The tree could have fallen the other way and the house could have suffered substantial damage from the branches of the tree and the force with which it fell. The black car was a sorry mess, but her beloved house was unscathed, like it had been in the floods.

A familiar van cruised to a halt when it could travel no further up the lane and Rose could see that another van was pulling up in a similar fashion on the other side of the tree. Both vans looked very familiar. Ironically, both Steve and Tom had turned up at the same time to make sure she and the house were OK. Steve and Tom both had a soft spot for Rose. She was very sure that Steve was waiting for Tom to make a fatal mistake in their relationship so he could step in, save the day, and go out with her instead. Bizarrely, the men were firm friends since they met last year at the house. They both worked in manual roles, building and gardening, and had lots in common with each other. They even helped each other with finding work and routinely recommended each other's services to clients. Often when Steve finished an inside job, he passed the outside job to Tom and vice versa.

A little crowd formed on the village and the Captain's House side of the tree, onlookers tramped across her garden to get past to have a look at the other side, marvelling at the root ball of the old beech tree as they did so. Steve and Tom greeted Rose and both of them checked she was OK, giving her a hug. They then stood to one side in a little huddle with David, working out how to deal with the tree. They strode towards the outbuildings purposefully to retrieve their tools and clear the tree from the road, followed by others from the village keen to lend a hand. When they got back to the house, there was a Police car parked up alongside the outbuildings in the lane. Tom recognised the officer as the one that brought Rose home safely when Mickey had his accident. The officer called to Tom, "I have just been told that the lane is blocked by a fallen tree and that there has been an accident when the tree fell. Is an ambulance required?"

Tom replied, "Not sure, mate, I don't think so, I think the car was empty when the tree fell."

The officer nodded and then made his way on foot towards the crowd milling excitedly alongside the tree. Rose saw the uniform from a distance and walked towards the police officer, hoping to speak to him out of earshot of the crowd. She was anxious about the cost of the fallen tree and wanted to know if she was liable for the damage to the parked car. She was worried too about the occupant of the car and wondered if she should ask the officer to make a search of the area. Should she tell him about the scream she heard, or was she dreaming? No one else appeared to have heard a storm. They spoke about heavy rain when she asked them, that's all.

The officer was happy to explain the implications of the fallen tree to Rose and speak to her out of earshot of the crowd as well. He was often hampered by well-meaning members of the public while doing his job and he had already spied a local reporter taking photos and saw that the reporter was speaking intently to what was very likely his editor on his mobile. She decided to tell him about the scream but explained that she was dozing in bed at the time, avoiding getting up, so she was not one hundred percent sure that it was real or not. The officer informed his supervising officer on his radio when he had checked out the tree and the car. He then strode back up the lane checking to see if he had missed an injured animal or person as he did so.

Tom and Steve passed Rose and the constable on their way back to the tree with Tom's tree-cutting equipment. The constable was happy that he didn't have to call anyone else to deal with that part of the incident and happy that the road would be cleared as soon as practicable.

Rose found Val and David still with Christian and asked them all to come inside to warm up, dry off, and have a cuppa.

They left Tom and Steve in the rain, to clear the tree from the road. Rose was happy that she didn't have to tell them what to do. She hoped that they would use the fallen tree to fill the large gap in her hedge to stop everyone wandering into her garden. She was sure they would.

When the crowd realised that the tree was about to be cleared and they would either have to join in with the clear up job or disperse, they all started to drift away back to the village. Leaving the journalist on the scene with his camera, taking photographs from every angle, watching and listening all the while.

The rain continued to fall, and the job was difficult and unpleasant. Tom and Steve worked diligently and well together, an ideal team. It was a number of hours later before they joined the others at the Captain's House. By then, the road was deserted, the journalist had long gone, and the black car remained in the entrance way to the field, smashed beyond repair.

## Thirty-Eight

That week the local newspaper was full of the news of the demise of the ancient beech tree and that of the posh black car that had been a write off when the tree fell. If it had fallen the other way the outer limbs would have damaged the Captain's House, so the talk of the village was about how lucky Rose was to have missed disaster for the second year running. The newspaper had added a photograph of the house the year before with the flood waters starting some distance away and the house looking for all intents and purposes as if it had a moat surrounding it. The newspaper had not mentioned the name of the owner of the car and there was still speculation as to who owned it and what it was doing parked up there in the dead of the night. The police had towed the car away and, when Tom had made enquiries, he was told by the police that the owner had been informed and he had collected his vehicle.

Steve and Tom had looked around the property for any signs of forced entry or criminal damage the night before the tree fell. Mickey had popped up to the folly to check that it was still locked and secure. No one disbelieved Christian, but they couldn't find any evidence of any foul play that night, however hard they looked.

As the weeks went by, Rose was a little blindsided by the storm that she had experienced that no one else remembered. The bad weather was blamed for the tree's fall, with prolonged snow, rain, and wind. A wet winter with no time to dry out. Rose had seen a couple of walkers give the other large trees a shove as they went by on the borders of her property to see if they were standing firm. The old oak on the footpath to the folly was tested this way by Mickey several times over the last week. Mickey joked that all his dogs always had a wee up that tree, so it had never dried out for the best part of sixty years! Rose wanted to blame the weather, but she wondered if her captain had anything to do with the tree's mysterious fall and if the storm was of his making. Was it his way of making her safe? The captain certainly seemed to be making his feelings known recently. She loved the fact that he seemed to be looking out for her but was growing increasingly uneasy about what he was warning her about and protecting her from. The threat existed in her world. Her life. She had no clue who or what was coming for her, or why.

She didn't want to worry Tom with it all, but she had managed to cajole him into staying with her ever since. She was making him very welcome, pandering to his every need, anxious for him not to leave her alone in the house with her seemingly belligerent captain. It was a complete turnaround for Rose who normally relished the time in the house by herself, enjoying her good fortune and making plans for the future. This time when Tom left for work, Rose either popped up to see Val to have a chat and a cuppa or wandered into the village for a newspaper and walked home via every conceivable local footpath and every which way. She popped into Mickey's to watch him bake the infamous 'throw in' fruit cake and taste his first ever homemade cake. She drove into the local town, visited coffee shops and florists. She even journeyed over to London to visit her old office and have a chat with Sarah, who had taken over her old job. She timed her returns to coincide with Tom's and she was hardly ever at home on her own.

The first person that had the courage to call her out on her odd behaviour was Steve. He was still popping around to finish the odd jobs around the house and the outbuildings and he missed her company. Rose made time for Mickey and Val in her days, so they wouldn't suspect a thing, but Rose had forgotten about Steve. He had not forgotten her, nor had Mowzer who was constantly under Steve's feet, causing havoc as he was desperate for some attention during the daytime.

Steve was working in the dining room at the front of the house and had seen Rose pull up on the driveway. He strode out to meet her, then opened her car door and dropped into a deep bow. Rose joined in with the charade and pretended to be a princess to his prince and curtseyed low once she was out of the car. Hand in hand they headed to the back door and Steve turned the door handle to let her in. The kettle was at the boil, so Steve made them a cup of tea while she busied herself putting her groceries away and stashing the biscuits away at the back of the cupboard out of Tom's sight so he wouldn't be able to find them. They took their tea into the back room and Steve set about lighting the fire for the evening. He knew he only had a short period of time before Tom was due in. He turned once more to face Rose, who was curled up in the armchair with her tea perched on the arm, cooling until it was ready to drink.

"Rose, I hardly see you these days. Where are you dashing off to all the time? I am starting to think you are avoiding me," Steve said.

Rose looked up and was startled to see Steve staring at her intently, waiting for her answer, "I have had a lot to be getting on with, you know how it is," she replied.

"Really, Rose, are you going to use that one? Really? I think you are avoiding being alone here. What has happened? You love this place, Rose! At one time, we all had to pressure you into leaving the house, just for a quick drink in the pub, but now you are rarely here! Come on, you didn't even set a date for your own studio open day, you kept thinking about a date and then procrastinating, this is not like you. You are leaving it all to Tilly and Dotty. Come on, tell me."

"You really have got the wrong end of the stick; I can't stay here all day every day you know!" she counteracted as she sat up sharply, spilling a puddle of tea into her lap. With a yelp she jumped up and rushed into the kitchen to grab a cloth to dry her jeans with. Steve waited at the fireside for her return. She didn't return, so he went to find her.

There she stood leaning against the kitchen worktop, with her head in her hands. Steve gently took her hands away from her face. He pulled her into him and put his arms around her and held her tight. She let herself be held tight for several moments and then took a deep shuddering breath and pulled away.

"There is something odd going on in the house right now, I feel I should know what it is, but I don't. I don't like being here by myself anymore, so I go out when I know I will be. I know we keep missing each other, it's not personal, Steve."

"Have you told, Tom?"

"No, I haven't had to, he doesn't know as he is not here much during the day. He hasn't noticed. I guess you have caught me off guard as I forget you pop in during the day when your other jobs allow. You are so good to me."

"Ah, so I caught you off guard? You think it is only me? Everyone has noticed you are always out and about these days, but nothing is getting done with your big studio idea. This is a small village, and you have lots of friends, surely you didn't think you could pull a stunt like that, Rose?"

She searched Steve's face to see if he was telling the truth. His face said it all. He knew precisely what was going on and so did all her friends.

"I really think you should tell Tom everything, Rose," he said, giving her another big hug.

"Tell me what?" said Tom as he entered the kitchen. "Tell me what?"

# Thirty-Nine

Steve had accomplished exactly what he wanted. As much as he wanted to talk it out with Rose, he was not daft enough to hang around. He grabbed his coat and, with a reassuring grin at Rose, he looked straight at Tom, "Over to you now, mate. You can see she is upset. Look after her. I am sure you can deal with everything. If you need me, you know where I am, call me." Steve let himself out of the back door and headed for home.

Tom rocked back on his heels and held his arms out for Rose. She fell into his arms with a sigh. 'Two guys in less than five minutes, what am I like', she thought to herself until her train of thought was halted by an answering sigh from another female voice. This time, unlike before, they both heard it, and both looked in the direction that the voice was coming from. There was no one there.

"Did you hear that?" Rose asked Tom, even though she knew he had as he had turned in the same direction.

"Yes, I heard that, it was almost like there was an echo, but this is a kitchen. What is going on? I have heard another female around the place for a while now. I think it is you and it's not. You are not far away. Sometimes there is a shadow, alongside you."

They both looked down at the kitchen floor and sure enough there was a slight shadow off to the side of Rose. Rose emitted a nervous giggle and sure enough another giggle followed a short time after. Tom looked at Rose closely and could see a tear trickle down her cheek, a sob caught in her throat. The shadow alongside her grew darker and larger and the sound of another woman sobbing could be heard, very quietly. Barely audible.

Rose leaned hard into Tom. He stood there with his arms around her, taking her weight, his hands slowly stroking her hair. He felt a pressure against his back and a breath in his ear. Rose was leaning against his right ear, but the quiet breath was exhaling into his left ear. Rose also felt a tickle against her cheek and the scratchiness of facial hair. A gruff cough sounded in the darkness and a deep voice penetrated the sobbing, "Be calm, my love. All will be well soon. I will take care of it all, my love."

Rose and Tom continued to hold each other tight. Tom was oblivious to the man's voice for he could only hear the quiet sobbing. Rose heard the now familiar voice that seemed to whisper in her ear when she needed him. It was not the comforting voice of the Captain that she dreamt off last summer, nor was it the voice of the Captain she had caught fleeting glimpses of since she lived there. This voice was new, not as comforting as it was less familiar. Was it another captain that had lived in the house that was now whispering to her? What did this captain want and why did she feel less reassured with him in the house? Was it the voice of the Captain that might have kissed her in the folly or was that Tom?

Rose pulled away from Tom and resolved to tell him everything, like Steve wanted her to. She was sure that they needed to find out what was threatening her and her home and then things would calm down. Her earlier resolve that had deserted her for a few short weeks was back, she was going to stay in her captain's house and now was the time to sort her new business out too. She put it all into words curled up beside Tom on the sofa in front of the fire. She told him almost everything and started to plan once more for the future, but before Tom could answer her …

"That's it my love, that's it," a familiar voice answered instead, although only Rose had heard him speak. "Well done!" he went on.

## *Forty*

Rose felt better after confiding in Tom. She felt really silly when he told her exactly the same as Steve, that everyone around her knew she was out of sorts and was concerned about her.

Tom was giving her time to work it out herself. He was only too pleased to be wanted, loving the extra time he was spending in the house again. He loved independent Rose but liked Rose to lean on him too. He was cross that Steve had confronted her before he had thought to do so. He was good friends with Steve, but also knew Steve had a soft spot for Rose and wouldn't put it past him to try his luck if Tom gave him a chance to do so. He hoped that this wasn't the chance that Steve needed to get ahead in her affections. Coming in and seeing her in Steve's arms was a real shock to the system, and seeing tears from Rose had cut him to the quick.

Rose didn't discuss all of it with Tom, she just gave him a quick rundown of what was on her mind and where she was coming from. Her ghostly experiences with the Captain and the mysterious lady were just touched on but she didn't share everything with Tom. She was fiercely loyal to her captain and his advice remained personal and just known to her. She didn't share those few phrases with Tom.

She felt a bit disloyal to Tom when she realised that she wanted to talk it all out with Steve, not him really. Tom had interrupted the moment when she would have told Steve everything. Steve had been there at the start when she first got the house. He had always been there for her. As much as she loved Tom, Steve understood her feelings about the house and was totally on her wavelength. She didn't have to explain much to Steve, just a look would be immediately understood, she had felt comforted and safe in his arms. She knew she was developing a sweet spot for Steve, and she would have quite happily shared what the Captain had said with him.

It seemed that most of the village had been trying to find out the owner of the black car which had not been seen in the village or local area since. Tom reckoned it was because it was a write off and whoever it belonged to would have had to use another one. A worrying turn of events as no one would be able to identify this mystery man and his menacing behaviour could continue unhindered.

Being confronted into talking about recent events with Steve and Tom that day turned her mood on its head and enabled her to focus on her Open Studio Day again, which was still in the diary, although she had carefully tried to forget it for weeks. Tilly and Dotty had done most of the administrative work for her. Steve, Tom, and the other guys had shifted stuff around in her outbuildings and got the studios into workable places while she had been out and about. There was not much left for her to do. Val and Mickey had sorted out the baking and refreshments. It was invitation only, so there was no need for posters and adverts in the local press. Rose was planning to advertise later on if those people she had invited to look at the workspace did not take her up on the offer. She was hoping that everyone would. Some of those invited had asked to bring friends and other business owners, so she was hoping she had enough space and would not have to turn anyone down.

A Saturday had been picked as the most suitable day for the Open Studio. Everyone who had been invited had confirmed that they were coming. Rose was nervous but very excited that everything was coming together. However, this didn't stop her constantly looking out of the window when she was upstairs looking for a sinister car or a stranger. She tried to relax again in the house once more, spending time at home alone again.

Rose's friends popped in to see her frequently though. She suspected that Val had drawn up a sort of rota to keep her safe and as a way of keeping an eye on her. She was secretly pleased that everyone cared enough to do so and kept the tea and coffee flowing during the day for her friends. Steve was conspicuously absent at the house and answered Rose's messages and texts in his normal prompt manner, stating he was busy working on another property in the area. Rose missed him and wished he would make time for her.

## Forty-One

All Rose really had to worry about for the Open Day as the days passed was the weather, as everything else had been sorted out by her friends. The cold weather appeared to be behind them, and the promise of spring was just around the corner.

So, she had potted up some old chimney pots and other earthenware pots that she had found around the garden in a very old potting shed that was affixed onto the side of her 'utility' outhouse. It was full of ancient garden implements, old forks, hoes, spades, and a variety of pots in all shapes and sizes. It was a quick 'in and out' job for Rose as the cobwebs were massive and she guessed that they were probably inhabited by massive spiders and hundreds of their baby spiders too. She dusted the cobwebs out of the pots with a broom from a distance just in case and gave them a good wash to make extra sure.

Rose had bumped into the owner of the local nursery, Sam, when she was looking around his nursery site pushing an empty trolley. He teased her mercilessly that she was shopping for plants on her own without Tom. She explained that it was one of those impulse shopping trips that women are infamous for. Tom would have bought herbs or something structural, taking time to think of the shape and impact of each pot. Rose just wanted colour, just colour, not longevity or permanence. The ambience of her site with seasonal flowers scattered about in quirky pots made people smile and the place looked cared for and loved. She wanted people to want to work and spend time in her little buildings, a little extra floral encouragement wouldn't hurt. She needed to breathe some life back into the old place and she loved the idea of being surrounded by people again. Rose never ever believed she could miss the office environment, but it turned out she could. These people would be there on her terms as it was her property, her business.

Before the workmen had even properly started the renovations on the house last year, she had popped a couple of pots either side of the front door with spring bedding plants in them. Val had teased her mercilessly for doing that. She was doing the same with her outbuildings, before they were occupied as shared studios and workplaces. By the time she had finished there were lots of pots filled to the brim with flowers in a mass of contrasting colours, adding vibrancy and drama to the scene.

There were pots at the entrance to every building, on every step in the courtyard and the old mounting block in the yard. She had lined the drive with pots half hidden amongst the shrubbery and roses, flashes of colour that would catch the eye on the way to the house or the yard.

While she had been messing about in the garden, moving pots, and shifting them about to see where they looked best, she had had the feeling that someone was watching her. She had felt someone's gaze on the back of her neck most of the afternoon. Every time she turned around, there was nobody there. Sometimes, when she had turned a corner, she felt she had just missed somebody that had just turned another corner in front of her. It was an odd feeling, but she did not feel uneasy. Quite the contrary; she felt like someone was being mischievous, that they were keeping out of sight to be playful. She half expected to hear a giggle, a laugh. That companionable feeling that she had been used to and had been missing for a while had returned.

She was tired, covered in potting compost, and admiring her work when Mowzer trotted across the drive and proceeded to wind himself around her jeans, wanting affection and maybe a morsel of something tasty. That cat was always hungry. They heard the noise together, looked up in unison, and saw the shadow flit along the building directly opposite them. Mowzer took off at once to investigate and Rose followed. She turned the corner and there on the bottom step of the mounting block she saw a pair of brown boots flickering in and out of sight with Mowzer happily winding his way around each boot, as he had done moments earlier with Rose. The boots abruptly disappeared. leaving behind a very faint outline of a figure. Mowzer didn't care, he was too busy rubbing his little chin and body up and down the now non-existent boots, looking up in ecstasy. Rose was totally forgotten.

Rose smiled broadly at the antics of Mowzer and exhaled an involuntary 'aah'. As she did so, the figure reappeared just for a second or two, so she could make out a female figure sat atop the mounting block mirroring the actions of Rose earlier, reaching into the nearest pot filled with flowers at her side. Pushing the bedding plants into the potting compost and making them firm and upright in the soil. Her hands were dirty and as she reached down to fondle Mowzer's white belly and chin, she left little brown stains on the white fur. She returned Rose's stare and smiled broadly back before vanishing from sight, leaving an answering giggle lingering on the still air.

## Forty-Two

Tom woke Rose with breakfast in bed on the morning of the Open Studio, coming into the bedroom holding a big mug of tea and a plate of buttered toast. Tom held her plate of toast high in the air away from the inquisitive nose of Mowzer, who was balancing on his back legs, swiping at the plate with his front paws. Mowzer followed Tom from the end of the bed to the bedside cabinet and sat on Rose's face as Tom put the plate down.

She brushed the cat off her face with her hand and sat up to greet Tom with a thank-you kiss. Tom sat down beside her on the bed and stretched out to envelop her in a big hug. He kissed her cheek and was reaching for her mouth when she turned her head away from him, gazing over his shoulders to mutter sleepily, "What's the weather like, Tom? Is it a nice day? Is it sunny?"

With a sigh he got up without getting a second kiss and walked around the bed to draw the curtains and let the light of the day in for Rose. A sliver of morning light hit the room. It was still very early but there was a hint of sunshine in the light. A tease of a sunny day to come.

"Oh, Tom, I think it is going to be a nice day, maybe some sunshine as well. Do you think anyone will come? Perhaps I have wasted my time. Whatever happens I will never go back to work in London, I am going to stay here forever!"

"I am sure you want to stay there forever, Rose, but you really must get up soon. You wanted to get a head start with everything.

Although, to be honest, there is not a lot left for you to do. Val will be bringing the cakes over in a couple of hours and did I hear this right that Mickey has baked too? Something about a 'bake off' with you? Or have I been dreaming?" He shook his head with the craziness of it all and looked hard at Rose for clarification.

"I didn't mean 'stay in bed' forever, Tom, I meant that I will never commute to work again. I love the idea of working right here. I am not really 'working', just keeping an eye on everyone else working for the moment. Hmm, how nice is that?" She sipped her tea as she mulled her good fortune over once again in her head. She would never forget her Great Aunt Lily Anne Rose who left her this house. It was her life-changing moment, like winning the lottery but on a smaller scale, much smaller really, but just as life changing for her.

"Mickey has made a cake you know, we both have. A 'throw in' fruit cake we call it, it's his late wife's recipe and Val is going to judge it this morning when we cut it up for everyone to eat. Just something silly between friends. I didn't know I liked baking, but I do."

"If you have been baking, how come I haven't been eating the cakes for the past few weeks? Oh Rose, have they been so awful that you have been throwing them away!"

Rose chucked a pillow at him after that comment. "I suppose I did bin the first one, but I have been taking them round to Dotty at the shop for her opinion. She liked most of my attempts, taking the cakes for the rest for the family to nibble on, so there was never any left for you. You can taste some this morning if you like. I baked the last one to perfection yesterday morning. I am a dead cert to win you know," she said, reaching for a slice of toast to nibble as she smiled confidently back at Tom.

Tom was happy to see Rose back to her normal, optimistic self. It was not the time to tell her about what had greeted him in the yard when he had got up to make her breakfast in bed.

It was a sight that was so bizarre that, at first, he thought he was still dreaming when he looked out of the window. All the pots that Rose had potted and carefully placed around the outbuildings and along the driveway had been moved into one big mass of pots alongside the main building. There was no rhyme or reason for this as nothing had been damaged. There were no drag marks or any soil spillage anywhere. Some of the pots were heavy and would have been a two-man job to lift, as Rose had moved them empty and filled them in situ. Very strange. He thought that he would have heard them all being moved around and seen torchlight flashing as they did so. To his knowledge, nothing had been taken but the only person who could answer that was Rose, who was gazing up at him with such excitement for the day ahead that he felt terrible for having to spoil her day.

Tom waited until Rose was up, dressed, and downstairs, blocking the view from the kitchen window with his body as he gestured for Rose to go straight outside, taking the breakfast things from her hands and putting them on the draining board. She slipped her feet into her boots, grabbed her coat, and dashed into the drive. She looked around her with a smile. Looking back at Tom she pulled a face.

"What did you rush me out here for? It looks perfect. I love what you have done with all my plants and pots. You have such an eye for all things botanical and they look so much better where you have placed them."

Tom squeezed past Rose to see what she was talking about. There was no way that the ungainly pile of pots that he had seen earlier could look better than how Rose had placed them before. He took a deep breath and was ready to contradict her when he took in the scene for himself. The pots were not stacked up next to the outbuilding as they were when he had seen them earlier. They were in almost the same places as Rose had them before but arranged in groups, ever so slightly different but in an arty, bohemian way.

They had both been upstairs getting ready and organised for the day and everything had changed once again. Tom was startled but pleased that Rose thought it was him that had made the changes. He had not heard a thing and a job like that would have probably taken most of the morning and would have knackered his back completely.

"You are so strong moving those pots on your own, Tom. With not an ounce of mess anywhere, no wonder you are so popular with your customers. I should be cross with you for interfering, but I love you so much for caring. It looks so, so perfect now. Thank you."

She turned to him and kissed him firmly on the lips, putting her arms around his neck and drawing him close. A bewildered Tom kissed her back.

He took her hand and they walked over to the main outbuilding to get the doors open and start the preparations for the day.

The main door was unlocked and swinging in the breeze.

## Forty-Three

Tom slung his arm around Rose as they walked towards the open door. He wanted to keep Rose close as he was worried about what they were going to find. He slowed the pace and tried to maintain a slow shuffle to the door, so he could collect his thoughts and come up with a plan of action. When they reached the door, he was just about to step out in front of Rose and protect her from whatever was within when they heard the patter of paws coming towards them and the familiar snuffle of Bert as he walked. The Spaniel greeted Tom and Rose with delight and led them back to his master, Mickey, who was busy laying a bright, floral tablecloth on one of the benches underneath the window. He had baskets galore around his feet, Bert was not at all interested in Rose and Tom anymore and had his nose wedged in the baskets, trying to work out what was in them and if he could sneak a bite when no one was looking.

Tom was so pleased to see Mickey and that the interior of the building was just as he left it the night before, all set up for the day's event. He turned to Rose, "I wasn't aware that Mickey had a key to this building, Rose?"

"Yes, I gave Mickey our spare yesterday afternoon, so he could come and go this morning with his and Val's cakes and all the other bits and pieces that they were sorting out for me."

Unnoticed, Bert had continued his snuffling in the baskets and was proceeding to pull a strand of bunting from the biggest basket.

"How many cakes have you got with you, Mickey? There is a mini cake mountain, right here!"

Mickey turned and smiled broadly at the pair of them, "I have been baking, as has Val. We have cakes, biscuits, scones, Kentish jam, and even some Cornish clotted cream that I spied in the supermarket. Val is going to make up little platters of cakes and stuff, like you get for afternoon tea. She must be bringing the chocolate brownies to go with the coffee as I can't find any here. Don't forget to bring your cake in, Rose. Or are you waiting to make a grand entrance? It should look like mine though, as we had the same ingredients and weights and stuff. Although mine is going to be tastier than yours, without a doubt."

Rose laughed, "Mickey, how deluded you are, my man. My fruit cake is bound to be better than yours. We will have to wait and see what Val says, won't we? When is she due to arrive?"

"Any minute now," Mickey replied.

There was a crash as a basket toppled over and a triumphant whine from Bert as he managed to pull a bunting strand free from the bottom of the basket. He raced off, trailing the strand of brightly coloured bunting behind him. Rose grabbed the basket as the last of the bunting was let loose. Bert scampered off around the room at a brisk trot, winding the bunting around every chair and table leg as he went.

Tom gave chase which excited Bert even more. He started to bark and trot faster. Mickey stamped on the end of the bunting with his foot and brought Bert to an instant standstill as the bunting was firmly stuck around the furniture. Bert was just shy of the table when it started to topple. Tom grabbed Bert by his collar just as the table fell sideways, the table catching him on the hip bone.

Tom and Bert yelped together, Bert with dismay that his fun game was thwarted and Tom with the sharp pain from the corner of the falling table.

The outbuilding door rocked in the breeze and a hand came around the door to hold it open. Val stood there with her hands on her hips like a school headmistress. "What is going on here?" she cried. "You were supposed to be getting it all sorted, not creating a mess and wrecking the place!"

It was just like Val to appear at the sound of chaos, and she instantly regained order. She grabbed Bert from Tom and took his lead from the tabletop and tethered him to a hook just inside the doorway. She took the basket from Rose and gathered up the rest of the baskets from the floor and put them on the tables. With the flick of a wrist, she pulled the bunting free from the nearest table leg and started to wind it back into a ball.

"Proper little Nanny McPhee, aren't you, Val!" Mickey chortled. Then grinned at Rose, "I know you thought I was of the era to say Mary Poppins, but I know my children's films and Nanny McPhee knocks the socks off Mary Poppins."

"You need to watch your tone, Mickey, my love. Cake tasting, or should I say judging, is in just a few minutes, well as long as it takes Rose to put the kettle on, if she hasn't switched the urn on in here yet?"

"We have just arrived, Val," Rose replied. "You switch the urn on, and I'll get our mugs from the house, give me just a sec!"

She hurried from the building and returned to the house, closely followed by Tom.

"Rose, wait Rose, you need water in the urn first, silly. Wait a bit, you will need a hand. I will take the water jugs and you can bring the mugs and everything else. Oh, don't forget your cake, Rose."

When Rose and Tom finally returned to the outbuilding after several trips, they saw Mickey's cake proudly displayed on one of his best bone china plates. Rose still had hers in an old tin that she had found in the back of the pantry.

"Presentation, Rose, my dear," said Mickey, "presentation is everything. I feel I have won already."

Not wanting to feel outdone, Rose raced back indoors to her house and dived into the pantry where she had found the tin. Right at the back was an old plate, one of many that were stacked in cupboards around the place. The plate was propped up right at the back. It had a fancy pattern and it looked like gold leaf on the rim. She reached in and unwedged it with her fingertips and carefully brought it back into the light. It was a dull grey with accumulated dirt but when she ran her finger over the edge, she could see that it was supposed to be a white or creamy colour. Taking a damp cloth from the sink, she wiped it over several times and then ran it under the running tap. The plate was stunning and perfect for her cake. There were tiny roses running around the rim in gold leaf making the roses stand out from the plate. In the centre were two initials intertwined. She didn't have time to look to see what initials. She ran back into the building with the plate under her arm and produced it with a flourish to everyone inside.

"This is style, Mickey. Just perfect for my 'perfect' cake."

Tom reached out and took the plate from her. "Definitely perfect but looks antique and could be worth a bit. Where did you find this? Not sure you should put your cake on this. I would ask Phyllis to take a look at this today while she's here."

"Really, Tom, a plate is made to be used, don't be silly." Rose took the plate from him and carefully placed her fruit cake atop.

Mickey tried to disguise a smile and Val gave a nervous laugh. "You are both taking this too seriously now. It is meant to be fun!"

## Forty-Four

They all held their breath as Val cut into Mickey's cake and took a very small slice. She did the same to Rose's cake and then placed both cakes side by side. She looked at the texture, moisture and even bent down to sniff each one. She pulled a couple of pastry forks from her jacket pocket and laid a fork down alongside each slice.

"Are you ready?" she announced, and with a flourish as she took a forkful from Mickey's slice. Without betraying a hint of emotion, she took a small sip of water from a water bottle she produced from the other pocket of her jacket and then picked up the clean fork and took a taste of Rose's cake. Replacing the fork alongside the cake, she took another sip of water and gazed thoughtfully up at the ceiling. She noticed a couple of stray cobwebs in the corners and watched the dust motes swirling around in the sunlight above the window. She was taking her time. It was really too close to call, and she was debating what to do about this as she knew that each of them desperately wanted to win. They would not share the prize, not that there was a prize. Just that one of them had to win, that was all, she supposed. She could call in someone else for their opinion, or she could call it.

Rose, Mickey, and Tom watched her intently, looking for any visual clues as to what she was thinking and who might have won. Bert sat at Mickey's feet and watched Val too, his little body quivering in excitement and confusion. The Spaniel could feel the mounting excitement in the room too.

A few moments passed then Rose couldn't stand it any longer, "Stop spinning it out and being a drama queen, Val. Put us both out of our misery please. Who has won, whose cake was best?"

Val gave a massive sigh and then gave a deep meaningful groan, "This is almost too close to call, as they are both bloody fantastic. If I really have to call it, I will say that Mickey has just pipped you to the post, Rose. By just a tad, a very weeny tad. The cake was a little more moist and yours was a touch more dry. A personal opinion. It's like splitting hairs."

She grimaced and pulled both of them into a hug, laughing as she did so. "I don't want to be the judge anymore, you know!"

"I think the best person won and an even better person came second," said Mickey graciously.

"I never expected to win," Rose exclaimed with a smile. "You have eaten that cake for years and it is so special to you. I am so glad you can make it for yourself now! What an achievement, your wife would be so proud of you."

"Iris would have been gobsmacked. Speechless, and believe me she was rarely lost for words! Thank you, Val, you have made my day. I reckon she would have loved you, Rose. Loved you for trying so hard to make her cake and for looking after me." His eyes started to well and he wrung his hands together and stared at the floor in a vain attempt to stop anyone noticing his tears.

Of course, Rose noticed his tears. She reached over and held him tight in her arms, looking past his shoulder at the door incredulously. Tilly and Joe had arrived with armfuls of what looked like more cake boxes. The studio was turning into a cake shop before a guest had arrived. Not a bad thing, a girl can never have too much cake!

Joe was a workaholic and everything he did, he did at a fast pace. He was used to being in charge in his restaurant, so he took charge here as well. Within minutes he had the two fruit cakes sliced and under glass cake stands. He had opened all the cake containers and tins in the baskets and was arranging them artfully on the side, making sure they were appropriately covered so Mowzer could not get to them, and they were far away from the table edge so Bert could not sniff or sneak a crafty bite. He had brought cutlery and crockery from his restaurant.

Rose, Val, Mickey, and Tom stood back and just watched him bustle about like a busy bee on a summer's day. Tilly had disappeared several times to her car and reappeared with more boxes and paraphernalia. She beckoned Rose back to the table and got her to look inside another box. Rose did not look fast enough, so Tilly reached in and brought out a cloth napkin with a drawing of the house and the words 'The Captain's House' embroidered underneath it. She waved it under Rose's nose. "A gift for you from me. I had them made up. You have twenty napkins, a couple of hand towels and these." She reached into another box and brought out a mug with the same design on.

"I thought we could use these in the studios, to make us feel more inclusive and welcome the others to the 'team'. Obviously, I am already here and on your team. I am just waiting for you to ask me to sign on the dotted line and give me a date of when I can start working here. I have my business name and accounts set up and just need to hand in my notice when you give me the OK. Sometime soon, I hope. I want to be my own boss and work right here. As I am first, can I pick my space?"

Rose could see why Joe and Tilly got on so well as they were both cut from the same cloth. Organised and focussed. What a shame they did not have the right mix of skills to work together. It was Joe's loss and her gain.

"Oh wow, Tilly. Give me just a minute to catch my breath. Of course, you can work here, you didn't have to wait to sign the official stuff. Hand your notice in now, if you like! There is always room for you here."

Tilly punched the air and grabbed her phone from her bag. She went silent and tapped at the phone frantically. Her excitement was infectious and even Joe stopped what he was doing to watch. Then, with a piercing shriek, she dropped the phone, crying, "I have done it, handed in my notice. I am officially my own boss!"

## Forty-Five

It didn't take long for all of them to sort the rooms of the outbuildings out between them. There was no rush and they had plenty of time. Tom went to check that the urn was working and at the same time made everyone a cup of tea or coffee. Tilly was beside herself with excitement and was perched on a chair in the corner with Joe alongside her, telling him all about her plans for the future and the space. Her chattering filled the room and the bake off was forgotten. Joe had sliced their cakes and set them at opposite ends of the big table. They were so similar that no one could tell them apart on appearance. Everyone had a small slice of both, and agreed that they tasted remarkably similar, but that was to be expected as they were baked to the same recipe.

Val regaled them with tales of the cake competition at the village fete in years gone by. The same recipe was used then, but the cakes varied hugely. Local ladies had fallen out for years over the Victoria sponge cake and fruit cake competitions. Mickey knew his wife would always be first in the fruit cake stakes in his eyes. She made the competition fruit cake but preferred to bake her own recipe the rest of the time. She was never the type to fall out with anyone. She chattered to strangers and would befriend anyone and anything. Much like Rose.

Rose had managed to creep out of the building without anyone noticing. She had stuffed a piece of cake into her pocket, wrapped in one of her new napkins, and she held a mug of steaming tea in her hands. She headed for the old bench in the garden that she went to when she wanted to have a moment to think. She wanted to savour the moment of the day, the day she had been procrastinating about for so long. There was nothing to worry about anymore, the day was here. People would either want to work here or they wouldn't. If they didn't, she would have to come up with a plan B. She was still waiting to hear about the Captain's paintings that she had discovered not long after she moved in, they were supposed to be worth a fortune, but their provenance had yet to be proved. Bridget and Chris, Lisa's parents, were dealing with this for her. She really should ask them how they were getting on. The paintings had been returned to her and were on display in the local museum in the meantime. If they were worth a lot of money then Rose would be in a good financial situation, but she couldn't help but think that her luck was bound to run out before long. She had an amazing inheritance from her Great Aunt already, she wasn't going to be greedy and want anymore. She would make what she had work for her, anything else was a bonus.

She sat on the end of the bench and placed her mug of tea alongside her, tracing the inscription on the back of the bench with her fingers. 'I venture across the seas, but always return to you.' She loved this sentiment, it fitted so well with the house and all the feelings that were wrapped up in it from the people who had lived and loved there in the past. Her ancestors, her family, and her beloved captains. She knew there would have been more than one captain that had lived in the house and the events of the past few months had confirmed this. The captain that she had glimpsed on this bench with Tom was not the same captain that she had heard since the events of Christmas, whispering to her and getting close. The captain that she felt belonged with the bench was linked to his hat. The captain that she felt in the folly and that now whispered in her ear was different. Totally. Now she understood why the Captains' manner had changed, realising that there were more than one captain in the house, the folly, and the outbuildings. She was much more accepting. More comfortable.

The 'whispering captain', as she thought of him, had evoked his lady. A new presence in the house.

She sipped her tea and munched her cake, thinking of all the captains that had owned and lived in her house and what their lives would have been like. She felt happier than she had for days as she sat in the warming late winter sunshine and let herself relax. Feeling the warmth of the sun on her face she closed her eyes. The bench tilted a little and gave a little lurch. It tottered slightly. One of the wooden slats lifted slightly against her leg. She felt a pressure next to her thigh. Without opening her eyes, she smiled. Was that a captain sitting down beside her?

## *Forty-Six*

Rose sat with her eyes shut basking in the sunshine for several moments. She had no reason to open her eyes and look to see who had sat down next to her. There was the tangy smell of tobacco smoke and the quiet inhaling puff of a pipe. She felt the brush of a tip of a tail on her hands which were holding her mug. She was resting her mug on her legs to keep it steady. Mowzer was winding in and out of her legs and the legs of her companion, purring loudly. The weight next to her shifted slightly once again, she felt a small tap on her shoulder and what felt like an arm behind her head. She leaned to the left into her companion and put her head on their shoulder. She felt warm, loved, and protected.

Impulsively, she opened her eyes and turned her head to take a look. The presence vanished instantly. Rose toppled to the side, put her hands out to save herself, and threw the contents of her mug all over her legs. She scrambled to her feet, throwing her mug on the grass as she did so, narrowly missing Mowzer who had dashed across the grass to avoid a shower of hot tea.

Steve rushed across the grass to her aid as he had seen her topple from the driveway where he was parking his prized Triumph car.

"Are you OK, Rose? You seem to have a habit of throwing tea over yourself whenever you see me!"

Rose was still unsteady on her feet and couldn't believe that she had spoilt it all by opening her eyes. She looked down in dismay at her soaked smart trousers that she had taken ages to choose that morning. The smart black trousers that matched her smart black suit jacket and her red knitted jumper. Even her jumper had splatters of tea on it and her trousers were ruined. She had wanted to convey the businesswoman vibe to everyone, which is why she had dressed that way. She only had one other business suit, but that was a summer weight suit and would be too chilly, even if she was dashing in and out of the yard to greet everyone.

"Rose, stop looking like that! It is only a set of clothes. You always look nice in whatever you wear. More than just nice sometimes."

"I don't want to look nice; I want to look right! I have nothing else to wear!"

An infectious giggle came from the other side of Steve's car where Dotty was just getting out. "Surely, you have something else to wear. It is an open day; people are not here to suss you out. It's the workspace and the building they are nosing around in. You are incidental, if you like. You are sussing them out and seeing if you want them around the place. Don't wear your heart on your sleeve today, girl. That's what I am here for. Your right-hand woman to set you straight."

She marched across the lawn and took Rose's arm. Steve passed Dotty the now empty mug from where it had landed on the grass. He nodded at Dotty and they both shared a knowing smile. Rose knew when she was outnumbered and meekly followed them back into the house. The last lingering whiff of pipe smoke hitting her nostrils and making her sneeze as she did so.

Steve busied himself in the kitchen, making Rose another cup of tea and one for him and Dotty too while the girls went upstairs to hunt for another outfit in her wardrobe. He was standing at the sink and watched Tom making his way back to the house, having realised that Rose was missing. He raised his hand and waved at Tom as he got closer.

"What are you doing in here and why are you washing Rose's mug? It only had tea in it a while ago, she should be still drinking it." Tom didn't come inside, he stopped just short of the kitchen by the back door, indignant that Steve knew where Rose was. He was miffed that Steve was standing at the sink looking very much at home.

"Quit looking at me like that, mate. Rose spilt her tea in the garden and has gone up to change into something else with Dotty. She was worried she had nothing to wear." He raised his eyes to the heavens as he did so. "Seriously, mate. What are you looking at me like that for?"

Tom couldn't help but be suspicious of Steve; there he was, in Rose's kitchen again, as if he owned the place. At least Rose wasn't in his arms like she was the last time he saw him in this kitchen. He hadn't seen Seve since then, not in the village or at other jobs. They often bumped into each other out and about, but Steve had been conspicuously absent for a while. Rose had not mentioned him either, that gave him the right to be suspicious.

Steve turned to face Tom, "Surely you don't think that ..." His words tailed off as he saw Rose behind Tom, with Dotty following on behind her.

She had changed into her smart black jeans and a fleecy shirt. She still wore her smart black boots with a substantial heel. She looked more like herself and felt more relaxed. Both men thought she looked very sexy. Had the Captain instigated the change of clothes in his inimitable way? Rose wouldn't put it past him, at all.

## Forty-Seven

Dotty picked up on the tension between the men, but Rose didn't. She didn't help matters by rushing to Steve and giving him a big hug.

"You always arrive at the perfect time, you do. Another cup of tea as well. What are you like!"

Tom stood to one side and inwardly fumed. It was not the time to say anything. He was friends with Steve, but maybe that wouldn't work in the future, as he was not sure he could keep a lid on these feelings for long. There was no way that Rose would stop being friends with Steve though, or was she already more than friends with Steve? Why else would she spill her tea when she saw him parking up. Did Steve bring Dotty as a cover?

Bizarrely, Rose was thinking about Dotty arriving with Steve at the very same moment. Were they getting close? Could they be together? Rose felt slightly jealous as she would always have a soft spot for Steve, but her heart was with 'her' Tom as she stared back at him. When Tom looked back with an almost murderous look in his eye, she was shaken to the core. She blinked rapidly and took another look. His expression had changed, and he was 'Tom' again. 'What brought that on?' she thought. She gave him a nudge and pushed him out of the door toward the outbuilding for the second time that day, leaving Steve and Dotty behind to make their own way in their own time.

Halfway across the yard, she tugged his arm to get him to stop. She turned him to face her and asked a direct question, "What was that look back there, Tom? You looked like you wanted to murder someone. What's got into you? Is there something wrong? Talk to me."

"If you would give me a chance to answer, Rose, then I would." Tom was unsure whether to tell Rose right now, when everyone would be arriving fairly soon. He didn't know how she would react. He had no time to think of something else to cover his feelings up, so he just answered her from the heart, "Well, Rose, I am not sure if you have something going with Steve, you know. I keep finding him in the kitchen, the last time with his arms around you and this time making himself very much at home. You got something to tell me?"

Rose took a step back and counted to three in an attempt to control her temper. She got to one before she started to talk, "I don't believe you men sometimes. Is that all you think about? Women can have friends that are men you know, good friends. If you start turning into Mike, I will scream, I will really—"

"I loved it when you screamed my name, Rose," a familiar, nasally whine answered her, full of sexual intonations. They both swivelled on the spot.

There was Mike, leaning against the bonnet of a very swanky brand-new car. He raised an eyebrow sardonically at Rose and Tom. His car was parked at an angle, blocking the way for anyone else to get into the yard, as Mike never thought of anyone else but himself.

"Trouble in paradise, sweetheart?" he sneered at Rose. "Regretting your choices, darling? I am here to make it better. I have been watching your pathetic attempt to make a success of your ridiculous idea for these buildings, my partner and I have much better ideas, so I want you to take a look at my proposal. Stop all this nonsense and listen to reason. Did you really think I would just toddle off into the sunset when you have this little goldmine right here? You need me to help you with this, not your thick country types. Really, Rose, you can't decide between a gardener and a 'run of the mill' builder. My Rose had more taste. She had me."

Steve and Dotty had heard all the commotion and joined Tom and Rose in the yard. Tom and Steve were united in their hatred of Mike and things were just about to kick off when Dotty marched towards Mike, to everyone's amazement, with a smile playing on her lips and a definite twinkle in her eyes. Steve held his hand to shield his mouth and whispered, "Aah, I think she is up to something."

She stopped in front of Mike and gestured with her hands for him to stand up. "You can't think she would consider business with you slouched over that car of yours like a pile of crap! You said you had a business proposition. How did you intend to discuss that with Rose? Did you plan to get her in bed? Really, I hope you have some paperwork prepared?" She leaned over him, copying his mannerisms to the letter, giving him a firm taste of his own medicine. He stood up straight and stepped away from Dotty, clutching the wing of the vehicle for moral support as he sidled to the driver's door and reached onto the passenger's seat through the open window. He picked up a sheaf of papers encased in a cardboard glossy folder with a name in bold fancy type emblazoned across it. Without a word he passed it to Dotty. Then he went to open the driver's door to get in. Dotty caught the top of the door frame with her other hand, "Where do you think you are going so fast, don't you want to discuss it with Rose? I am sure you planned to, didn't you?"

"I don't need to discuss it with Rose, she knows it is a good idea. It's been a cold, hard winter here for Rose. She has been unhappy, just as I predicted she would be. Odd things have happened here, haven't they?" he said with a knowing smirk. Brushing Dotty's hand off the door, he slammed it and proceeded to execute a flashy three-point turn in the thankfully empty yard. He took off down the drive, spraying gravel from behind his spinning wheels and intentionally spraying gravel over her new pots and the lawn.

Speechless at his antics, they stood and stared as the flashy black car drove away.

## Forty-Eight

---

Val was walking around the gatepost towards the house from the lane just as Mike left the driveway, she had to practically jump into the yew bush to get out of his way. She clambered from the bush just inside the boundary hedge when he had passed, pulling bits of yew from her jacket.

"Who the hell was that?" she yelled, scowling as she walked back up the drive. "They all but squashed me like a piece of fruit on its way to being fruit bloody squash!"

Rose and Dotty ran to meet her. "You alright, Val?" shouted Rose, absolutely astonished at the turn of events from her peaceful interlude a short while earlier sat on the bench. She was so shocked to see Mike again. Like everyone else, she thought he was gone for good after the last time he was here … to think he nearly knocked poor Val down on his way out.

"I am alright, really I am. I might need a quick sit down for a bit. Good job I have finished with all the bunting, which is looking fantastic on the hedge outside. Something to let everyone know that they have arrived at the right place. Tilly told everyone to park in the lane by the bunting you see, as there would not be room for everyone in the yard or up the drive to park. She wanted to give everyone the illusion of lots of space in the yard. She reckons that if everyone signs up to work here, no one will be all working here on the same day, or very rarely, so the yard will still be perfect, but no harm in giving the right first impression, is there?"

"Will there be room for people to pass though on the lane, Val?" said Rose, worried that she was going to be unpopular with the locals.

"Yeah, I am sure there will be unless that idiot decides to drive down the lane again as recklessly as he drove away from here. Who is it and why was he in so much of a hurry? I didn't get a look at his face."

Dotty roared with laughter and replied, "That was me giving that idiot a taste of his own medicine and giving him the creeps for a change. He is not used to an assertive, sexy lady like myself, he scarpered as soon as I breathed on him. What is he to you, Rose?" Dotty implored. "Please tell me he is not your 'ex', is he? Surely you had more taste. I know he is very easy on the eye, but really!"

"Afraid so, Dotty. In my younger and very stupid days, I hasten to add," Rose replied, shaking her head sadly.

"Much more sensible now," she added with a grin at Tom, who was now standing beside her."

"Thank goodness for that, Rose. You wouldn't have been made so welcome in the village if you had that prat of a man with you. I bet his plans for this place wouldn't have gone down as well either." Dotty brandished the glossy brochure in the air before passing it to Rose. "At least we know what he is up to now he has given you this to look at."

With his usual wry grin, Steve added, "Yeah, let's have a quick look before we use it to light the fire with. Let's see his plans for this place, I wonder if they include you, Rose, maybe? I bet he has offered you a large cash sum for the entire property, or he wants you to be another business partner as well as trying to get you to be his girlfriend again too."

Val stretched out her hand for the brochure and Dotty passed it across to her. She peered at the name on the front, trying to make out the name without her glasses. "We have enough to do right now, this can wait. I reckon he came up here deliberately at this time to put us all off our stroke. We all need to focus on the open day, not on his stupid ideas or him. Stick to your original plans, Rose, and forget him, and this, until later."

Reluctantly they had to agree with Val, and they followed her back into the outbuilding like a row of ducklings following the mother duck. All apart from Tom, who had made a detour back to the house, grabbing the back door keys from the inside of the door and locking the door firmly. He even gave the handle a little shake to make sure it was locked. He didn't trust Mike not to sneak into the house while everyone was busy. He really didn't trust him as far as he could throw him. Tom didn't trust anyone at the moment, not even Steve, who was supposed to be his friend.

Joe and Tilly were still ensconced in the corner when they got back. Tilly had an A4 notebook at her side, her laptop open, and her phone to her ear. She had planned this moment for a long time and was already making a start. Joe was mesmerised by this change in his girlfriend and was listening intently to Tilly's conversation on the phone. When she had finished, the pair of them looked up, suddenly realising that everyone had left them, that they had been gone awhile and they had all returned seemingly in a bit of a tizz.

"Where have you all been? Val, why is your cheek scratched? Rose, have we got a first aid kit here?"

Joe looked at Tom, "What has been happening? Please don't tell me all the women have fallen out? Did I miss a catfight? There's something about girls fighting, isn't there?"

Tom grimaced then grinned at his brother's words, "Take your mind out of the gutter. You should be worried if they have all fallen out. Where would Tilly run her business if this place was out of the picture? Eh?"

The main door behind them squeaked as it was pulled open from outside. A tiny voice exclaimed, "Hello? Is it OK if I come in now?"

## Forty-Nine

Rose opened the door wider and looked out. The voice belonged to Pearl, a larger-than-life lady, dressed in a very bright orange dress. She was clutching a large handbag and an A4 notebook in exactly the same design as the one Tilly was already holding. She was wearing a pair of staggeringly high heels in a matching shade of orange. She was definitely dressed to impress, having the same mindset as Rose earlier, when confidence is needed just increase the size of the heels, but, unlike Rose, she added a confident colour too! Her clothes giving her much needed confidence as she was really very shy, and she almost sneaked into the building when Rose opened the door. Seemingly frightened of her very own shadow.

"Are you open yet? Can I come in and look around? I just need a space to meet my customers and lay out the samples for my customers to try. Can I come in yet? I am a bit early, but I wanted to get in first, as I am sure lots of people are wanting to work here." She had practised her opening lines before arriving, but her nerves were making her words run away with her.

Her shyness was very appealing, and after wedging the door open to welcome everyone else that was due to arrive shortly, Rose led her to the furthest corner of the building, away from Tilly and the others, to try and put her at her ease.

"Of course you can come in. Come and sit down and make yourself comfortable. My name is Rose. Would you like a cup of tea or coffee to start with?" she said as she put her hand out to shake Pearl's hand.

"I am Pearl, pleased to meet you too," replied Pearl, shaking Rose's hand. "Oh, you are so kind, but I would love to have a look around before it gets busy you see. I assume you have more than one room or office, but I am happy to share." She cast her eyes around the room, "This is not 'it'. I need somewhere more cosy, smaller."

Rose led her through the next few rooms, chattering about her requirements and answering her questions as she did so. When they had left the room, Tilly jumped up like a 'jack in a box' looking for the first aid box to treat Val's scratch that was beginning to ooze droplets of blood. She needed some antiseptic wipes and time to have a good look at it. The first aid needed to be administered in double quick time before their first 'customer' came back and explanations had to be made.

The ladies made quick work treating the small wound that the vegetation had made on Val's cheek. It was not a deep cut, but it was similar to a paper cut or a razor cut which seems to bleed forever before it stops.

Two ladies arrived together next. A complete contrast to Pearl, who was still in one of the back rooms with Rose. They were both dressed in paint-splattered trousers and looked as if they had just rushed out.

"I had completely forgotten it was today when the Captain's House buildings were open, I rushed round to Ashley's on the way, and she was merrily printing in her shed, oblivious to the date too." She proffered her hand to the nearest person, who was Dotty. "I'm Sue. I paint landscapes mostly, but I need lots of space as my canvases are big. That's my signature trademark I suppose. Bigger than everyone else. Takes longer too. Ooh Ashley, we have come just in time. Look at the array of cake. Fruit cake, my favourite. Ooh two fruit cakes. A cake for you and another one for me. What do you reckon, one each? A whole one I mean." Finally, she paused to take a breath.

Ashley took her moment, "Oh my goodness, I am really not sure I can work with you chattering on so, but I do get so lonely all on my own in my shed. It gets a trifle cold out there too in the winter months, even with the heater going full pelt. Plenty of space to keep out of your ear shot, I reckon, so I should be ok." She strolled around the big table that Rose had placed in the centre of the room with work benches outside. "That big table could be shared if you needed it somewhere in a 'process'. What a terrific idea. Take your eyes off the cakes, Sue. Come and have a look."

As Ashley and Sue walked around the huge table which took up most of the room, Rose and Pearl came back into the room. Pearl was aghast at the lively chatter and that there were even more people in the room than when she left. Rose was surprised as even though there were now loads of people in the main room and tables awash with cakes, the space was still not filled. It still felt huge and spacious, and light flooded the room through the large windows and the open door.

"Bet you need that tea now, Pearl," she said encouragingly to Pearl, sensing her trepidation at having to meet new people.

Ashley and Sue, still trailing their fingers over the tactile surface of the wooden table, looked up and they both smiled at Pearl. "Oh, my goodness, you are Pearl? You are the amazing lady that can cook anything and caters for all the posh ladies. I saw your feature in that glossy magazine when I was taking my cat to see Dale, the dishy vet in the village, and had to wait ages as someone was keeping him chatting, probably that Phyliss who thinks she is in with a chance. Bless her. Has anyone told her he is gay?" Sue paused for another breath, still smiling broadly, and offering her hand for Pearl to shake.

"So pleased to meet you. If we work together, can I offer my services as 'chief taster'? Your stuff is said to be the best in the area, with the exception of our Joe here of course. No comparison really as you have to go to his place and eat in his restaurant, but you cater for private events and take your food out to important people. Wow, oh wow!"

Rose looked from one lady to another. This was make or break. They would either hate or really like each other. They were like chalk and cheese. The whole room took a breath ,waiting to see how this would pan out.

## *Fifty*

Pearl and Sue exchanged glances and then burst out laughing. Pearl's was a tiny tinkle of a laugh and Sue's a giant guffaw that filled the space. They laughed together, not at each other. It looked like the start of a friendship. Everyone smiled at their laughter, and it broke what was left of the proverbial 'ice'. Ashley was secretly thrilled that Sue had another avenue for her constant chatter.

Tilly, the youngest woman in the room, watched the older ladies with amusement and trepidation. Older ladies liked to 'mother' her and she had enough of her own domineering mother without having three more to add to the mix in her new workspace.

The men quietly filed out of the room holding cups of tea in one hand and napkins filled with cake in the other. Joe followed Tom and Steve next door into Rose's utility room which could only be accessed by an external door. It was getting too much for the men, all the women. They needed to vacate the space and fast. As they piled into the room next door, they discovered that someone had got there before them. He was perched on a stool holding what was left of a cream and jam scone in one hand. Bert was at his feet, looking grumpily up at the intruders who had awoken him from his late morning nap. There was a selection of cakes on a couple of plates in front of Mickey on the work surface, next to a folded pile of Rose's clean washing that was waiting to be ironed.

"I was wondering when you lot were going to join me and how

long you could stand it in there. Did you miss me? What have I missed?"

The others pulled up chairs and made themselves comfortable before telling Mickey all about Mike's visit and the potential new occupants of the outbuildings. If the conversation lagged, they could hear Sue's big loud voice and her even louder laugh from the other side of the wall. The rooms shared a large beam running through the building and there was a small gap around the edge, which was all that was needed for the sound of Sue's voice to travel.

"That must be Ashley's artist friend, Sue, that I hear loud and clear. She is so much fun, salt of the earth, but knows everyone's business and everyone can't help but know hers. Mike won't be able to sneak about if she's here. Neither will Rose for that matter. Should we tell Rose or let her work it out for herself?" said Mickey.

"I think it will do Rose good to have some regular company here during the working week. She can stipulate the hours the buildings can be used and negotiate any use outside of those hours. I agree Mike will think twice about coming around if the yards full of cars and there are other people about. It may change the feel of the place for Rose, she will have to share this bit. I wonder how she feels about this. The way to tell is if she comes in here looking for an escape or looking for us!" Tom said.

Steve nodded his agreement but didn't add his opinion, partly because he had a mouth full of cake and partly because he didn't want to antagonise Tom anymore. It was easier and safer to keep quiet for a bit and let Tom simmer down. Tom looked ready to punch him in the kitchen earlier and he wasn't the sort to fight over a woman. He never usually had to.

The door was flung open, and all the men jumped as Rose flew in through the door and slammed it shut behind her. "Shush you lot.

What are you all hiding in here for, and with all this cake?"

A sea of guilty faces looked anywhere else but at her as she stood there with her hands on her hips. "Really guys, really! Mickey, I need you out there to meet and greet people, and Steve, Ashley wants to know if a bench is sturdy enough for her printing bits and pieces. Tom, I need you right there by my side, you know. Come on, guys, get a grip!"

She opened the door wide for the guys to come out, no one moved until she threatened, "If anyone wants to stay in here, please feel free to wash up the dirty mugs and make a start on my ironing pile." She waved in the general direction of the ironing board to add some clarity, but it was not needed. They all pushed past Rose in their haste to get out before she could get to the ironing board, just in case she was being serious. Rose giggled at the thought of Mickey ironing her clothes and turned to follow them.

As the men traipsed around the building, another man was coming the other way from the footpath, taking a shortcut through the hedge. He had to be a local for him to be aware of this shortcut.

## Fifty-One

Mickey was delighted when he recognised Dennis. Dennis was an old friend of Mickey's and another regular of the now defunct local, The Ship. They had not seen each other since the pub shut and they greeted each other warmly. Bert jumped up at Dennis, focussing on his right trouser pocket, using his nose to track the treats that he knew were there. They were for his wife's dog. Bunty was a qualified hearing dog and went everywhere with Shirley, who had dropped Dennis off for the open day in the car. Bunty was out working at the supermarket with Shirley resplendent in her burgundy hearing dog uniform. Bert did not expect to see Bunty without Shirley but was happy to snaffle Bunty's treats in her absence. Dennis and Mickey had bonded over beer, their love of dogs, and the fact that their dogs were brother and sister. Bert and Bunty were from the same litter, but Bert didn't make it as a fully qualified hearing dog, he didn't have the steady temperament needed. He was just right for Mickey and was rehomed by the charity, Hearing Dogs for Deaf People, as a sound support dog for him shortly after his wife died. Bert was a big comfort to Mickey in his grief and when he was having to cope alone in the house without his wife. Mickey didn't realise how much he relied on his wife hearing sounds for him until she passed, but Bert took on some of her roles – waking him up, telling him if someone was at the front door, and keeping him safe by alerting him to the fire alarm.

The others made their way back to the barn and left Mickey and Dennis catching up in the yard, as they were both so thrilled so see each other. Neither of them seemed to know where each other lived or exchanged phone numbers in the past to keep in touch. They never needed to as, until the pub had closed, they met almost daily at the pub. They both took their dogs to Dale, the local vet, so could have found each other if they had wanted to.

Mickey led Dennis into the main building and introduced him to Rose who was standing by the door waiting for the last few guests to arrive.

"Rose, this is Dennis, a very good friend of mine. His wife has got Bunty, you know, Bert's sister. You may have seen the pair of them around the village as Bunty wears the distinctive burgundy uniform of a working hearing dog."

Rose smiled but shook her head, "No, I don't think I have. I love dogs so I would have surely noticed. Are you here to look around?"

She looked around for the guest list and laughed as Dotty shoved a clipboard almost up her nose.

"Ah, my list tells me you are a photographer. What kind of space are you looking for here? An office or a working space? Or exhibition space, maybe? I had not thought of that but there would be plenty of room here to do something like that at a later date."

Dennis looked around at the light and airy space and smiled approvingly. "This looks fantastic, but can I see some of your office space as well as working space? I am here because Shirley, my lovely wife," he added quickly, "wants some of her house back and I fear I am taking over the space with my equipment and photography paraphernalia. I need somewhere nice to meet my clients without taking over the front room when Shirley is watching the telly. She loves her soaps does my Shirley."

"Follow me, let me show you around. Would you like a cup of tea or coffee first, maybe a slice of cake before the ladies finish the lot!" she giggled at Sue, Ashley, and Pearl who were huddled together in a little semi-circle tucking into the cakes, chattering incessantly all the while. Pearl was smiling broadly from ear to ear, all her nerves forgotten.

There was a barely perceptible frown from Dennis as he made his way past the ladies after declining a warm drink for the moment. "Please tell me, Rose, it's not all women wanting to work here, is it? I am making the move to get away from a woman's influence and get some peace you know."

Steve overheard Dennis's last comment, saw the frown form, and butted in, "I know what you mean, mate! Did you know that I have an office here, as does Tom?" He waved at Tom to come over and join him. "George and James, an electrician and plumber, also work in these outbuildings too. It's where we store our equipment, tools, and stuff. We often pop in before and after jobs to use the office to manage the admin for our businesses as surprisingly the wi-fi connection is brilliant here, unlike in the village and the countryside. We are always coming and going. Don't worry, mate. It won't be all women, I can promise you."

Steve and Tom walked over to where Rose and Dennis were standing, and Steve touched Rose's arm lightly to get her attention. "Think we will take it from here, Rose. Leave Dennis with us, we'll put him right."

Thankfully, Tom didn't notice Steve touch Rose's arm, all thoughts of animosity were forgotten as they took Dennis off to look around the other rooms and potential office space. They were gone a short while and then announced that they were going to have a quick look in the neighbouring building which was not quite finished. As an afterthought, Tom said, "Rose, would it be OK to show Dennis where we do all our admin and stuff next door?"

Pleased to be asked, Rose agreed instantly, but then wondered what Steve and Tom were up to as this building was entirely theirs and she had not thought that they would want to share it with anybody else. There was more than enough room in the main building for Dennis, but he would have to work near the 'girls'. She didn't see why this was turning into an issue.

Bemused by the turn of events, she made to follow them; after all, it was her land, her business. Steve unlocked the door of their building and motioned Dennis to step inside, switching on the overhead light. "This looks perfect for my office needs. A bit tacky, a bit scruffy, but it wouldn't take long to sort it out. Where does that door go?" he gestured at a door in the far corner.

Rose answered, keen to state her authority and take charge of the conversation, "The room is empty, it has another external door on the other side so you can get to it from the end of the yard. Tom uses it for his plants and stuff before and after his jobs, it's not the office space you are looking for." She wanted to keep this bit separate for Tom, so he had his own space that was his alone, without him sharing unless he wanted to.

She didn't know why she didn't want him to share with the others. Was it because they had taken it upon themselves to show Dennis this building and it wasn't her idea? She could feel herself getting cross with all of them. She turned on her heels and barrelled into a very tall lady who was standing in her way, peering with delight into the guys' office.

## Fifty-Two

The tall lady was immaculately dressed in a well-fitted navy-blue designer business suit. It looked expensive, everything about her looked expensive. She carried a large holdall and was carrying a big bottle of what looked like whiskey wrapped up in a twist of tissue paper with a big bow. The paper was bright pink, as was the bow.

She peered past Rose and rushed into the office. Rose looked back into the office, wondering what she was up to and who she was rushing to see. She was incredulous to see that it was her Tom that she was making a beeline for. The woman shoved the bottle into his hands and proceeded to kiss him firmly and loudly on each cheek.

"Oh, my little cherub. Thank you so much for what you have done to my garden. It looks fantastic, absolutely beautiful, and it sets the house off perfectly. When my husband got home yesterday afternoon, he was thrilled to bits with it all and was so sorry to have missed you again. He insisted that I come over this afternoon and drop a bottle of his finest malt whiskey from his private collection to you. I picked this one, because I liked the shape of the bottle and thought you could use it for a candle holder when it is empty. I used to do that when I was at university, until I met the man of my dreams, he educated me and told me it was rather common. I have never done it since, but always threatened to when he makes me host these rather dreary dinner parties for his business partners and investors. I put my design stamp on it you know, with the paper and bow. So, it looks fabulous as a gift for you. He loves my wrapping skills, he does. My darling husband. Loves unwrapping my naughty surprises in the bedroom." She gave a coquettish giggle and blushed, almost the same shade as the paper.

Tom was also blushing a deep shade of crimson; he was embarrassed by all the attention and wanted the floor to open up and swallow him.

With a stutter, he introduced her to everyone. "This is Judith everyone. I have been working on her new garden over the winter months, which is why you have not seen much of me. It was a big job and took longer with this awful weather we have been having lately."

"Oh Tom, you can call me Judy, now the job is done, my love," she proffered with another flirty look in his direction.

"Hi, there. My name is Rose," said Rose more forcefully than she really had to, "I am sure Tom has mentioned me. This is the open day for my business premises."

"Yes, that's another reason why I am here, I am here to have a look around for my husband, although he has an office and a study in our new house. He rather likes the look of the place here and wants to keep business and pleasure separate. I am here to have a nose around on his behalf." She put her hand around Tom's waist and gave him a squeeze.

"Tell her how generous he is and how tenacious he is when he wants his own way." She lowered her voice to a husky whisper, "He would pay at least triple of what you would ask I reckon, if I sold it to him right." She gave another squeeze of Tom's waist and slowly brought her hand across his buttocks then back to her side. "He can't work where I am as I am too distracting, but then you wouldn't see much of me, Tom, which is a real shame."

Tom and Rose exchanged a bemused wide-eyed stare. Rose was

thinking fast and on her feet the words 'at least triple', and 'he wouldn't see much of me'. Too good to be true, surely.

"Judy, why don't you come and look at the building next door and have an afternoon tea with me. We can pick a selection of cakes to go with our tea, instead of scones, clotted cream, and jam if you prefer?"

"Ooh, an afternoon tea, that would be so nice. I was popping into town for a new dress after this, but I can't resist a nice afternoon tea. I can tell you more about what my darling husband wants in his office."

Rose steered Judy across the yard and into the main building. Joe had just finished plating up some scones, with jam and clotted cream, so Val only had to add a couple of teas. With a nod from Rose, she brought out a couple of cups and saucers too and popped it all on a tray for her.

As Rose turned around, looking for a place to sit, Tom sidled up to her, and said, "Why not take her back to the house with your afternoon tea? I have just unlocked the back door. I think 'her darling husband' would probably prefer that workspace that Dennis had taken a fancy to as it has its own entrance. It wouldn't take long to get it smart. Charge them more than triple for it. I can find somewhere else in the yard. This is a brilliant opportunity for you to make this more affordable for the likes of Sue, Ashley, Pearl, and young Tilly." Tom spoke in a barely perceptual whisper that Rose had to strain her ears to hear.

Rose didn't like taking advantage of people, but she was never one to look a gift horse in the mouth. She steered Judy back out across the yard into the house for a quiet chat. Not sure if she could manage the hard sell that Tom was implying she did, she just resolved to get to know the woman who had Tom working so hard over the last few months. She wondered if Tom had charged her more than triple for his work!

She took Judy through the kitchen and into the back room overlooking the river and looking out onto the folly in the distance.

"What a view, my darling, this little part of the world is so nice. My husband just loves it so much too. So much that he says he wants to leave a bit of him here, bring the area into the future and leave the past far behind!"

As no one was in the house that morning, the fire had not been lit and the room felt a bit chilly. There were just the white dusty embers of last night's fire in the grate. Rose brought a little side table in from the dining room and put the afternoon tea on the table in front of them. She set about adding jam and clotted cream to her scone. She was just adding some more cream to the scone when the Captain's hat fell from the mantlepiece onto the floor with a clatter. Judy jumped out of her skin and knocked her scone, knife, and cream off of her plate and onto the rug below. The captain's hat had landed by Judy's feet, so she picked it up off the floor. Rose picked up the scone and attempted to scrape most of the cream off the carpet and left the room, looking for the wet cloth she had used earlier to sponge off her clothes. Another spillage, already. It was a day of spillages.

She was rinsing the cloth under the running tap, trying to remember when the hat had fallen last as it was so long ago, probably before Christmas, when she heard Judy yell. As she came back in, Judy was cradling her hand against her chest with her other hand.

"Hope that's a cold wet cloth, Rose. Look at my hand." She raised the palm of her hands with her fingers outstretched at Rose. The tips of her fingers and thumb were red and blistering.

"I picked up that hat and it burnt my fingers where I touched it – look." As they watched, as fast as it had blistered, it had started to heal. They both watched as the redness faded together with the blisters until it was no more. It was completely gone.

## Fifty-Three

Judy could not believe her eyes and kept staring at her hand. Rose looked around the room for any other reason why Judy would have burnt her fingers when she wasn't there. She looked across at the fireplace and gasped when she realised that there was a lively fire burning in the grate where before there was just ash. Neither Tom nor Rose had time to clear the grate and lay it out ready to light in the late afternoon like they normally would, as they had both focused on the open day that morning instead.

The flames crackled and spat around a big wide log that had burnt right through in the middle. It looked like it had been burning all afternoon. There was a branch of green foliage at the back of the fire which was giving off a spicy aroma as it burnt. Herby and sweet smelling.

Judy had not noticed there was now a fire burning in the grate, for she was not watching and listening to anything else. She always focused on herself and nothing around her. Judy was mesmerised by her fingertips and thumb, searching intently for any damage. She sat back down on the sofa, speechless at the turn of events.

Rose got down on her knees and scrubbed at the rug with her damp cloth, rubbing the cream and jam residue away with the wetness of the cloth. She kept a watch on the fire and on Judy all the while. Realising that Rose was completely disinterested in what had happened, Judy was bewildered. Did it happen or did she just imagine it did?

Rose took the cloth back to the kitchen along with the bits of scone and jam that she had picked up off the rug. She then went back in and joined Judy on the sofa again, putting one half of her scone on Judy's plate so she had something to eat. Rose didn't want to leave her alone again in the house while she nipped across to get another one from Val. She didn't understand what had happened. Judy was silent at her side now, her incessant chattering hushed by the turn of events. She was nibbling the edges of the scone and gazing out of the window at the folly just visible in the distance. Several times Judy took a breath as if to say something and then she thought better of it and remained silent.

Rose watched the fire burn bright, not sure if the heat in the room came from her embarrassment or from the flames. It was then she noticed that the pile of paperwork alongside the sofa was looking untidy, as if someone had been rummaging through it. An unopened envelope was at a strange angle just underneath a couple of folders. She had been going through that pile the evening before, sorting out unopened mail which was usually utter rubbish or random business circulars. Some of it was still addressed to her old aunt, attempting to sell her wide-fitting shoes or fancy cardigan sets. Some of it was the same stuff that had previously been addressed to her aunt, with just the name updated to the newest occupant, her. Tom called it her 'old lady post' and they both enjoyed the joke whenever the post arrived. She was sure that she had not left anything unopened last night. Nothing at all.

Could Judy have been snooping while she was out in the kitchen, was she looking for this envelope or had she put it there? Rose just wanted to get rid of her so she could find out. She wasn't worried about her hand or keeping her sweet or even charging her triple for an office rent. She wanted her out of her house, the sooner the better.

"Perhaps you had better go home, Judy, if you are feeling a bit out of sorts? Are you sure you would be OK to drive? Do you want me to call you a cab or I could ask Tom to run you home?"

Rose held her breath and prayed that she did not choose the final option, it was not that she didn't trust Tom, she wasn't sure that she trusted Judy anymore and didn't want her anywhere near 'her darling', she thought, inwardly giggling the fact that she had nicked Judy's 'darling' catchphrase.

"Oh Rose, I think you are right, I do feel a bit strange and although my fingers look and feel alright now, I think I should pop into my nail lady on my way home and ask her to take these gel nails off and give my hands a good pamper. I had them done on the way here, you know. She was new to the job this morning, but she won't survive until this afternoon when I make my complaint!"

Rose was horrified that some poor girl was going to get into trouble because of what had happened in the house. She did her best to come up with a viable excuse. "You may have had an allergic reaction to the hand creams, gels or something. Did you use anything different in your morning routine that could have reacted with their stuff?"

"Well, now you come to mention it, I did use that expensive bottle of hand lotion that my darling husband got me for my birthday last week. It smelt so lovely, so I used loads. You could be right. I suppose I will never really know, will I? You are so nice you are. I would have had that poor girl sacked, but I won't now. I will give her the benefit of the doubt. My darling husband says I am too soft sometimes, so I am trying to be tougher."

Rose walked her to the door and out to her car. She was going to ask Judy which car was hers as they walked down the drive to the lane, but she wanted to see if she could guess. There was a red convertible parked miles away from the edge of the lane at a crazy angle.

"That's my ride over there, Rose. My little red car. You put my name down for the external office and I will send my man over to look at it another day and sign all the paperwork for you."

Judy looked back at the house and the outbuildings up the drive, she gave Rose's shoulder a squeeze before she walked away, "Not sure I could live there. Evil house. Needs razing to the ground and rebuilding if you ask me," then tossed her long blond hair over her shoulder as she walked away.

Rose folded her arms tightly around her as she felt a sudden chill and walked back to the outbuildings to check on the open day, popping into the house to check on the fire first.

The fire was still burning merrily in the grate and the room was cosy and warm. The envelope that she had seen earlier was still sticking out at a crazy angle from the paperwork pile. She worked it free from the pile and stuffed it in her jacket pocket to look at later.

She placed the fireguard around the fire and picked up the Captain's hat from the arm of the chair where it had been left by Judy. She fondled it with her hands before popping it back on the mantelpiece.

Puzzling over the events of the afternoon, she wandered back to the outbuildings to see how everything was going. Firstly, making sure she shut and locked the back door on her way out and, secondly, checking her pocket for the envelope, making sure it was still there.

## Fifty-Four

Rose had spent weeks procrastinating about the open day. She was so very worried that no one would like or want to work in her buildings. Despite being out of the village with no passing trade, it seemed that her buildings were still extremely popular. The workspace could and would be shared, and a little community would be created as a result.

Not everyone turned up, but those that didn't had called Tilly on the day to schedule an alternative appointment to view the workspace. Remarkably, everyone who had attended wanted to use the space to work in and the final arrangements just needed to be tweaked to suit all the individual's requirements. Lots of brilliant ideas had been bandied about to make the space even better and Steve had a long list of jobs to do as a result.

Now someone else had shown an interest in the little room with its own front door, Tom was excited about the space and wanted to use it as his own, leaving the shared office to Steve and the boys. At least that's what Rose hoped. She wanted all the animosity between the guys to be gone.

As she and Tom snuggled down in bed together after their busy day, she mulled over the differences between Steve and Tom, sleepily comparing the two. Although she fell asleep in Tom's arms she was thinking of Steve when she dropped off. Steve was so dependable and reliable. She had never had a cross word with him. Tom was very similar, but when he cast a sultry look her way she was lost and was incapable of rational thought for a short while. As she rested her naked body close to his, exhausted from a busy day and satiated from an evening of passion that she really didn't think she had the residual energy for, she was thinking of another man, idly wondering what he was like in bed.

Mowzer crept around the bed and gently jumped onto the bottom of the bed, as not to disturb the slumbering occupants. He padded around in a circle first, then curled up tight to settle down to sleep.

The occupants of the house were all together, safe and secure, when the shadows appeared. A long shadow fell across Mowzer as he was sleeping, he opened one eye and watched as the shadow moved up the bed to the sleeping Rose. The shadow blotted out the moonlight that was bathing her features in a milky sheen and then crept across to Tom. The shadow danced across the bed for a while, before settling back over the watching Mowzer.

The fur ruffled up on the back of Mowzer's neck and along his spine. He started to purr loudly and lifted his head at the attention. As the shadow moved towards the open door, Mowzer leapt up and followed. His claws sounding a tapping beat on the floorboards as he trotted to keep up with the rapidly receding shadow until he could no longer be seen or heard, and the house fell silent again.

The shadow crept through the house and out into the yard, closely followed by Mowzer. The house was locked and secure, but for the tiniest gap left by the kitchen window not being put back on the latch. It was all Mowzer needed to squeeze out and follow his companion with a gruff purr resonating from the back of his throat as he prowled along. They wove along the edges of the buildings and, once satisfied all was well, meandered along the tracks towards the folly. The folly was hidden in the darkness as a cloud scurried across the moon, blocking the moonlight for a short while, but they knew their way in the darkness. Nothing else stirred in the countryside around them, it was as if everyone and everything was taking a deep breath in the darkness. It all seemed to stop for a moment in time.

Then the tower of the folly emerged from the dark, illuminated not by moonlight but by lamplight flickering around the base and the upper reaches of the tower. A solitary shadow paced the folly holding the lamp high above their head, peering into the blackness looking out to sea. The sea was hidden in the gloom of the night, the steady *ting, ting ting* could be heard in the stillness. Each ting getting louder and louder until a faint light could be seen in the distance, dancing from side to side then up and down. Side to side, up and down. As the light in the distance was dancing, the figure on the tower grew still, as did the lamplight. A breathy sigh hung in the air for a short while ...

When the moonlight broke through the clouds, Mowzer was curled up on the bench at the foot of the tower. Alone, one eye open, waiting.

## Fifty-Five

The success of the open day had prompted busy days for everyone. Rose was busy getting the legal documents sorted out for the business leases on the outbuildings. Tom was busy sorting out his 'new office' and the front door of his office was resplendent with his business logo. Steve was making the available workspace suitable for everyone who wanted to work there. Her new business venture was viable, and her outbuildings were now at full capacity. Those people that could not attend the open day had popped in shortly afterwards and bagged their space too, not wanting to lose out and wanting to be part of it. An air of optimism hung over the place. All thoughts of Mike were forgotten by Rose. His snazzy folder had been consigned to the rubbish bin the very same afternoon, without Rose even taking a peek. She had wanted to look but her friends had encouraged her to ignore him totally and not give him a moment of her time. If she didn't know what he had planned for her place she could not worry about it, she was told. This well-timed advice seemed to be working out for Rose and no one had seen hide nor hair of Mike since, thankfully.

Judy had not called again, but her solicitor had been in touch wanting to book some office space for her husband. Rose had tentatively saved some desk space for him but was not going to let him have anything without meeting him first. She wasn't sure about Judy, so she didn't dare wonder what sort of character her husband could be. It seemed strange that it was their solicitor that called her and not Judy. The solicitor was constantly ringing her mobile phone at all sorts of odd hours, looking for assurances that his client would have some space to work from in her building. She was heartily sick of it and was about to turn the business away when the solicitor stated that he was nearby so would call in that afternoon to see her in person to discuss the matter further.

It was very unusual that Rose was on her own. She seemed to have had a full house morning and night since the open day. People were calling in supposedly to congratulate her on her new business but really they were calling round to be nosy and to find out what the outbuildings were like inside and what all the fuss was about.

It was even more unusual to see the solicitor approach from the footpath that led from the folly. Rose had been crossing the yard from the house to the outbuilding in readiness for his arrival when she spotted him. He was not dressed for walking in the countryside. His smart, tailored suit trousers had been tucked inside a pair of obviously new welly boots, which still had the price tag dangling from the top of one of the boots. He was clutching a document wallet in his hands, around his neck hung a pair of binoculars and his phone was peeking out of his jacket pocket. It was his phone that he was reaching for when he dropped the documents onto the muddy yard. Yelling his dismay as they were all flung about in the wind, getting muddier and muddier, he answered the call and scowled into the phone and at Rose who raced into the middle of the yard to help him.

Trying but failing miserably to retrieve the situation, he concentrated on the phone call and let Rose attempt to catch the papers flapping around the yard for him. The papers that landed straight away in the wet mud stayed there but the papers that never made it to the floor sailed around in the breeze. With an exasperated sigh, he turned his back on Rose and her attempts to retrieve his errant paperwork and whispered into his phone. A familiar voice was heard by Rose, shouting at full volume on the other end. She could not place the voice or work out how she could hear him so well for several moments until she saw another man round the corner with his mobile held to his ear.

She stood and stared at both men in disbelief, all thoughts of collecting all the paperwork forgotten as she tried to comprehend the situation. She looked away from the men to try to regain her composure and down at the documents in her hands, the paper folder was smudged with mud and damp to touch, but she recognised it instantly. It was the same folder that Mike had pressed into her hands at the open day, but it was not Mike that was standing right there in front of her though.

She continued to stare as the man snatched the folder from her hands and continued to shout at the poor solicitor who was still holding his mobile to his ear in stunned silence.

With a loud disgruntled snort of disbelief of the turn of events, the man loomed over Rose like a rabid wolf in his deer stalker hat with the flaps covering his ears, waggling in the wind. He was so close that she could feel the front of his full-length Barbour coat tapping against her leg. She could smell his minty breath and his overpowering eighties aftershave.

What was he doing here, she wondered, and why had she agreed to meet a stranger when she was here by herself?

## Fifty-Six

Rose stepped away from Trevor and went to hand the muddied papers back to the official-looking man who was now looking just as scared as she felt at Trevor's side. The two men exchanged befuddled glances and shook their heads from side to side.

Rose looked down at the muddy papers in her shaky hands and saw a map of her land with the borders marked in a lurid pink highlighter and saw that the adjoining land was marked in a murky green colour, some of the borders overlapped into her land. Particularly the building that housed Steve and Tom's offices with the storage areas and over half of all the other outbuildings near to the house. The green encroached on several areas of her land and took a huge chunk from the other side of the stream along the footpath, including the folly itself.

Trevor let out a satisfied grunt and exclaimed, "Well, now you know, dearie. The land you thought was yours, isn't."

The solicitor cleared his throat with a nervous cough, "Good afternoon, Rose. My name is Mr Pernick, and I am working on behalf of Trevor here, who you appear to have already met," adding under his breath, "something else he hasn't told me."

He went on to say, with another nervous cough, "The plans that he has, along with his other properties, seem to suggest that this is the case. I wondered if you had any other paperwork that you can lay your hands on that would prove that this land belongs to you, as I am told you have recently been left this by an elderly aunt. My client seems to believe that this aunt of yours was not in possession of all the facts and some if not all of the outbuildings that surround us now and the land on the other side of this water here," waving his arms in the direction of the river, "including the place you call the folly, are in fact his."

Rose fought hard to hold back the tears that threatened to overwhelm her, sniffed hard and closed her eyes for a second, trying desperately to retain her composure. She took several deep breaths. She squeezed the papers tight in her hands and looked down at the yard. She was instantly crushed by the news and didn't know what to say to either of the men in response.

Trevor could not resist smirking at Rose's dismay, but Mr Pernick stepped forward and took Rose's arm gently, "Rose, is there somewhere we could sit down for a few minutes to discuss this further? I really think you should sit down."

"I am sure we could find somewhere to sit down in there." Trevor pointed at the door to the little office building used by Tom. "I have only got my wife Judy's word on what it's like inside, but I think she was dead right that it would make a fantastic site and sales office for the new estate that I intend to build on the other side of the river, with a luxury property to go in my half of the main building here. Fantastic part of the world this is, we already have a wonderful property on the go in the village, which is almost finished. Hard to keep you nosy lot out of the site, while it is being done, though," he sneered back at Rose.

Mr Pernick turned to the main outbuilding instead and beckoned Rose to lead the way. Dragging her feet, she did as she was bid and reluctantly pushed open the main door to reveal the new shared workspaces within. Rose and Mr Pernick entered together, and he pulled out a chair for Rose and sat down heavily in another.

"I am going to have a nose in the smaller building before I go inside," said Trevor, who was still standing in the yard and hadn't moved an inch.

"Have a heart, Trevor. Let the girl look at the paperwork first and get her breath back. Plenty of time for that another time."

Snorting like an angry bull, Trevor made his way across the yard and toward the door that had been left hanging open. As he drew level with the door frame, the heavy oak door slammed shut. The force rattled the window frames and everything else in the building. The noise of the slamming door reverberated around the building for what seemed like several long minutes.

Then there was a howl and a wail from the other side of the closed door. Mr Pernick leapt up and opened the door. There stood Trevor, with a torrent of blood running down his face from his spilt nose, forehead, and lips. His hands were fruitlessly trying to catch the blood from his bloodied face as it ran down his chin and his eyes were closed as he grimaced in pain. He started to hop from one foot to the other.

Rose grabbed a clean tea towel that had been left on the windowsill since the open day and approached Trevor with it. It would stem the bleeding for a time in the absence of anything else. Trevor staggered away from Rose, spitting blood in anger onto the floor.

He made an attempt to say something, but spat some more blood, missing the floor and sending splashes instead all over this pristine Barbour coat.

"Argh" was all that could be made out. Totally enraged and almost senseless, he waved Mr Pernick to his side and, holding onto the wall of the building to remain upright, staggered like a drunkard back around the building from whence he came.

Mr Pernick grabbed the tea towel from Rose and made after him, he turned to Rose as he was leaving, "Take a look at the paperwork and call me when you want to talk. I suggest you look at the will and property specifications you already have and call your solicitor. I will look after Trevor, don't worry about him for the moment."

As he hurried after Trevor, Rose stood aghast in the yard watching him leave. She hugged herself tightly and let a tear fall.

She wrinkled her nose when the smell of tobacco caught her senses. She flinched when she felt a light touch on her neck, but the weight stayed there and moved across to her shoulder as if someone was putting a comforting arm around her. She felt a breath at her ear, "Beware, I warned you. You have everything you need right here," then the words tailed off, lost in the breeze. A chuckle floated back, then a deep-throated guffaw.

# Fifty-Seven

The sense of the Captain standing with her halted the tears instantly, she set her shoulders against the world then she drew a deep, long breath and focused on what she needed to do. Mentally going through a checklist in her head so she could tackle Trevor head on. He had caught her on the hop, but not for long. She raged at the injustice of it all. Taking her temper out on the large heavy door of the main outbuilding when she slammed it shut and locked it, she stomped back across the yard and into the house through the unlocked door.

As she entered the kitchen, she cursed inwardly as she smelt the clogging smell of another familiar aftershave and saw yet another glossy brochure tucked under a plate of biscuits and a hot steaming mug of freshly poured tea from the teapot. Grabbing the mug, she took a few swigs, smacking her lips together afterwards with the heat of it. She took the brochure but forgoing the biscuits she headed for the back room. There, lounging on the sofa, was Mike, looking for all intents and purposes as if he owned the place. She looked towards the fireplace and saw that the fire was glowing brightly, and a new log had just been placed atop the embers of the logs that she had placed there before she left. She raised her hand into the air, which was holding the new brochure, shot a scathing look at Mike and went to throw it into the fire.

"Slow down, Rose," sneered Mike, "that would be really stupid of you. You need to take a good look at that, you know. That's why I am here, to console you and to offer you advice. You know I have your best interests at heart. Stop playing 'house' here. This is a valuable property, and you need to make use of its value in the real world. I will let you play 'house' with me somewhere hot and sunny. Not here is this dismal part of the world. You could build a house on a clifftop with stunning sea views, with all the trappings of our success, with the money you make from this deal."

He patted the side of the sofa beside him and flashed her his best sexy smile. "Rose, my darling little rosebud, sit down here and we will go through it page by page, petal. I will help you make sense of it all."

Rose could not believe that Mike had the gumption to just let himself in, make himself a brew, and get cosy in HER house. The fact that he had and was so at home frightened her. After seeing Trevor leave with a bloody nose, she had felt invincible. Had she imagined the touch of the Captain or his voice a moment ago? Was it just the wind that had slammed the door at that precise moment?

Why was she left alone once again, with yet another slimy visitor?

She was briefly at loss of what to do. She battled against her gut instinct to scream, shout at Mike and take him by the lapels of his very expensive jacket and drag him to his feet. Then drag him all the way to the back door and kick him into the mud of the yard. She didn't have the physical strength for that, but she so wished she had. Or should she just curl up beside him and cry those angry, bitter tears that were threatening to fall again and give in to it all.

Wrestling against her feelings she took the path of least resistance, as she lacked the stomach for anything more at that moment. She meekly handed the brochure back to Mike and gingerly sat by his side where he had patted the sofa earlier. She laid her head on his shoulder and looked beseechingly up at him.

"Oh Mike, what ever shall I do now?" she said quietly. "I have made big mistakes with this property. Tell me how to sort it all out and make it all go away."

Mike didn't need asking twice. He put his arm around Rose and pulled her into him, when she was held firm, he reached for the brochure with his other hand. He read aloud from every page to Rose in a slow, rhythmical voice. He cradled her in his arm like a parent reading a toddler a story before bedtime. Rose sat and listened without saying a word, without interrupting him at all. She sat processing all the information, sipping her tea all the while, then putting what was left on the little table and watching it go cold. She concentrated on the steam rising from the mug and, when that stopped, she turned her eyes to the logs in the grate, watching the flames flicker and fall. The wood turning various shades of brown, grey, and white as they burnt. The red glow of the hot heart of the fire. Time slowed as she listened carefully. Listened intently. As he turned the last page her concentration started to fail, and she drifted off to sleep.

Mike carried on talking, oblivious to the fact that Rose was fast asleep in his arms. It was some time before he realised. He got up slowly and carefully. He gently laid Rose against a cushion without waking her, then he took her mug back out to the kitchen and tipped her cold tea down the sink, washed the mug, and replaced the biscuits back in the tin. With a cursory backwards look at the kitchen, he let himself out of the back door and walked back down the drive to his car that he had left in the lane.

## Fifty-Eight

When she awoke, it was dark, and the fire was nearly out. Her neck hurt and her head pounded. As she massaged her neck in the darkness and tried to make sense of where she was, the standard lamp in the corner was switched on. The light hurt her eyes and made her head throb even more. She winced and blinked against the light but could not make out who had switched the light on until they came closer.

Steve crouched down to her eye level and looked her squarely in the eyes. "What are you playing at, Rose?"

"I am playing 'house' with Mike, you know," replied Rose sleepily.

"Bloody hell, Rose, house with who? The back door is unlocked and swinging in the bloody breeze. What are you playing at? Anyone could have got in. Luckily the movement switched the outside security lights on, and I could just make out the door swinging in the light from the lane. I was just going to pick Dotty up for dinner."

Totally bewildered, Rose stared at Steve. His familiar face was next to hers and all she wanted to do was kiss it. She drew in close and puckered her lips up to kiss him.

Then the overhead light was switched on, flooding the room with a bright light and illuminating the pair of them with Steve crouched down next to Rose with Rose leaning in close.

Tom stood in the doorway, his hand on the light switch. His face was fixed with a stern, forbidding frown.

"Please tell me that this is not what it looks like," Tom yelled at the top of his voice.

"Oh mate," cried Steve, "it is not what it looks like. We haven't time to fall out, mate. Something is really wrong with Rose. Look at her. Really look at her. I came in because the back door was open and swinging in the wind. Rose was out cold on the sofa; she is coming round but is not herself. She tried to kiss me, even though I have just told her I am going out with Dotty tonight, and I was on my way to pick her up. Oh my god, look at her, Tom. Her eyes are strange – all glazed."

Rose blinked at the two of them, trying to make sense of what they were talking about. She just wanted to kiss Steve and play 'house' with Mike. Or did she want to kiss Mike and play 'house' with Steve. Who was Tom and why was he looking at her like that? She looked around for something familiar and saw the brochure where Mike had left it. She shoved it off the sofa with her arm and sank back into the sofa again with a soft gurgle; she let herself drift off again.

Tom was not really registering all that Steve had just told him as all he could think about was had he really walked into Rose about to kiss Steve? When his temper ebbed, he rushed across to Rose's side and roughly shoved Steve to one side. Tom took a deep breath and was filled with concern for Rose

Tom cradled Rose in his arms, he told her repeatedly that he loved her, he really, really loved her and was never going to leave her side. Steve, being the pragmatic one of the two of them, promptly called her mum and dad and got them to drive straight over. He guessed that she was out of sorts again and thought her mum and dad would be the best people to get to the bottom of this one. Not him, or Tom, or any of her new friends, this time.

## Fifty-Nine

Despite Rose assuring Tom and Steve that she never took anything of the sort, a packet of over-the-counter sleeping tablets were found in the kitchen cabinet next to the kettle by Tom when he was making a pot of tea for her mum and dad when they arrived. There was another brochure with extra copies of some of the documents left neatly in a pile on the windowsill too. Rose had no recollection of how the items come to be in her kitchen. None at all.

Rose was adamant she had not taken anything. But the events of the afternoon were blurry. She was constantly bombarded with questions, which ranged from why the door was unlocked and left open to what the bloody stain on the outbuilding door was? She was uncharacteristically quiet, not answering anyone's questions and not talking about anything really. She kept everyone at arm's length.

Everyone was so worried about Rose, her mum and dad wanted her to go home with them for a while. Val, Mickey, Steve, Dotty, and Tom wanted her to stay at their houses too. It appeared that no one wanted her to be in her captain's house, but that was her home and where she needed to be. She needed to be here. She felt safe here, even though she had no recollection of the afternoon's events after Trevor and Mr Pernick had left. She only remembered that going back to the house and having some odd dreams, very odd dreams, and the next she knew the guys were shaking her awake and everything was a bit of a blur.

Rose was secretly hoping that she would remember everything very soon. She wished everyone would stop harping on about sleeping tablets and drugs. As if she would ever take anything like that, she was lucky that she had never had much trouble falling asleep and always slept like a log at the Captain's house. A big part of that was down to Tom, snuggling down and sharing a bed with him was conducive to a good night's sleep in every way.

She had to fight to stay in her beloved house this time as all her friends and family were urging her to stay away. She was having none of it. Absolutely none of it. It was her house and her decision.

Her mum promptly tucked her up in bed as she had done when she was a little girl and told her that she would have to stay there until the morning at least. Her mum told her that she was staying and was going to look after her. No arguments. Her dad was going home. She wasn't having any men there at all.

"I heard the squabbling from the pair of them this afternoon. Steve and Tom bickering over you. Well, I am not having any of that here, you need to rest and relax. Give the guys some space. I think Tom is a lovely guy, but he has practically moved in, hasn't he?" She picked up his work jacket and collected several pairs of Tom's underpants from the floor and went to peer under the bed.

"Oh mum, really," shrieked Rose, with her hand over her mouth to stifle a giggle. "You really mustn't look under there, you never know what you will find!"

"Oh Rose," she replied, sitting on the side of the bed, rummaging on the top of the bedside table instead. "I was hoping I was going to find a good paperback, but looking at your blushing face, I am guessing there is some saucy undies or such like under the bed, but I am hoping there is a packet of condoms as well, my girl" She continued to tidy the bedside table instead and lifted a cookery book to reveal a large packet of condoms underneath with only a couple remaining in the packet. Rose caught her mum's eye and they both started to giggle. The giggles turned into belly-aching laughs, making Rose and her mum hold their sides as they roared with laughter. It took several minutes before they were sensible again but still stray giggles continued to erupt. Satisfied that Rose was on the mend, Joan passed the cookery book to Rose and popped the offending box in the drawer of the bedside cabinet out of sight. When she saw that the book had caught Rose's interest again, and she had her nose buried in it, Joan made her way downstairs where Pete, Rose's dad, was patiently waiting for her.

"You can get off now, Pete. You must have heard the laughter. I think our Rose is on the mend now. I will keep a good eye on her and will stay here tonight with her. I am sure we will be alright, don't you?"

Pete waved the brochure at Joan that he had found on the sofa and shook his head. "I reckon this is what set our Rose off, making her want to sleep it all away. It all looks too dodgy for words, but I am going to take it with me and have a good look at this later on. I am not going home now; I am going to stay in the annexe instead. Val insisted on it. So I am not too far away if you need me. That cream tea has my name on it too."

"Rose is adamant that she didn't take anything, and those pills aren't hers and our girl is not the sort to lie. I can't make head nor tail of it all, but I will keep an eye on her and see you in the morning. There is another one of those in the kitchen with some loose paperwork, I will look at it this evening as well. Tom and Steve are popping over tomorrow, but hopefully not at the same time as I am not sure I can cope with them squabbling over what is best for Rose."

Pete gave Joan a fond kiss of the cheek as he left to head off to the annexe. He hadn't brought a change of clothes or anything, but he was sure he could make do for the night and Dave had offered him a loan of something of his to tide him over. Pete wasn't worried to much about clothes and toiletries for his impromptu overnight stay, he was far more concerned with the cream tea and the promise of a dinner with Val and David. Val's cooking was renowned, and Pete's stomach was doing the talking!

Rose flicked through the cookery book left over from the bake-off competition with Mickey. She knew her mum was right, that she would start to feel herself again in the morning. She was sure she would start to remember the events of the afternoon in time too. Not for the first time she wondered how it had all transpired, and where was her beloved captain throughout?

## Sixty

It was a real novelty having her dinner on her lap, but she insisted that she was getting up the following day. Rose loved her mum dearly but hated all the fuss. It all seemed so unnecessary as she didn't really feel ill at all, she just seemed to have a piece of time missing, that was all.

Her mind was still in turmoil and, as she waited for sleep to come, her mind threw random pictures at her of the strange carvings that she had found on several occasions since she had lived there. The carving on the window seat pointing the way to the folly that she had found ages ago and forgotten about until recently. The carving on the banisters that pointed to the outbuildings, in time for her to discover the leaky roof before it did any substantial damage. The same outbuildings that would be bringing in an income of sorts to allow her to stay in the house. There were marks everywhere which were all connected somehow, which seemed to show her the way when all was lost. The bells that sounded periodically; were they bell buoys being tossed around in the sea that could bizarrely be heard as far inland as the folly and the house? Or were the bells marking the time that had passed, like a ship's bell to show the passing of time at sea? The bells were the mysterious ringtone that had materialised on her phone. Was there a message in the bells for her? The giggles and the lady that appeared with them. The captain seemed to change with the bells. Was the passage of time changing with the bells? Could time cross over? Can captains change? His appearance, voice, uniform, and the warnings, the warnings ...

As her mind rambled, twisting and turning, she was too tired to make sense of the muddle and drifted off to sleep. Content and full after her evening meal, which her mum had brought up to her on a tray, she curled up in a ball and reached out for Tom to cuddle. She didn't have Tom in bed with her, so Mowzer had snuggled up close. He was pressed against her, snug between her arms and legs, right next to her tummy. His purring lulled her to sleep.

Her mum had fallen asleep on the sofa downstairs, snuggled up in a blanket in front of the glowing embers of the evening's fire. She had not made up the bed upstairs as although she shared the joke in the bedroom with Rose, she didn't want to overstep the mark and have Rose think she was nosing about in there too, making the bed up and looking for sheets and stuff. Rose was using the other big bedroom as a storeroom of sorts, storing some of the antiques which were found in the outbuilding renovations. Joan still found the presence of the figurehead that was found wrapped in a sailcloth in the loft space last year alarming when she was in the room. She always felt that the figurehead was watching her or moved when she wasn't watching. She would catch glimpses of movements from the corners of her eye when she was in the room with that figurehead. She was happier downstairs. Cosy and warm on the sofa.

All occupants of the house were safe and sound. Sleeping. Lamps appeared on every windowsill, burning brightly, keeping watch on the house. The sounds of rustling skirts with the soft footsteps of a lady filled the house and, in the garden, and the outside space, the heavy tread of work boots punctuated the silence while the smell of tobacco pervaded the air.

The stillness of the night was broken by Rose's jacket falling off the arm of the chair, waking Mowzer who promptly left Rose's side to follow the shadows once more, his claws clicking on the gravel and merging with the soft crunch of the manly tread.

The car sat some distance away from the house and the occupant within watched the house with binoculars fixed on the windows of the house. He could see that the windows were blazing with light, so it impaired who or what was inside. As he could not make out anything within, it was a wasted journey for him. There were no cars on the lane or in the driveway that he could see. He was tempted to creep up the driveway to make sure the house was empty and if he could sneak in. When he was last in the property he had checked to see which windowsill was empty and most of them were. No lanterns, lights, or candles. As he sat there completely bemused, the lights faded to a dull glow and the house was almost in darkness once more. The lights flickered and faded into nothing as the cloud rose to blot out the moonlight. In the dark, the headlights of the car flashed on and off. The hazard lights did the same. The interior light came on and temporarily blinded him, as the doors opened wide. The torrent of water came from nowhere, but the seawater filled the car with a foot of water which drenched the man inside. Then the doors slammed, and the water continued to rise until it was just under his chin. The man sat very still, too terrified to move. As the cloud moved slowly across the sky the moon light shone once more and the water was gone in an instant. The interior of the car was bone dry. The man within was not, he was soaking from head to toe, shivering with the wet and cold. He attempted to start the car. Surprisingly, it started first time and he drove away, completely unaware that the lights were burning brightly once more as he was totally uninterested in whether there was anyone in there anymore.

## Sixty-One

Rose awoke and crept downstairs to feed Mowzer and make her morning cuppa, trying hard to do so without disturbing her mum. She wanted to be up and about and not confined to bed for another day. She had managed to get washed and dressed so, so quietly. She was feeling much better and much brighter than the previous evening. While she was waiting for the kettle to boil, she came across the brochure and the sheaf of papers that she was given by Mr Pernick on Trevor's behalf. It was then that the full events of the afternoon came back to her. The fact that she was greeted by Mike, and he had gone through all the paperwork with her, explaining every detail, until he wasn't there anymore, but Steve and then Tom were.

She made a cup of tea for her and her mum and thought about it some more. There must have been more, much more. She reached for the biscuit tin to munch a biscuit and take some in for her mum and, as she munched, she searched for a plate, a saucer, anything to put the biscuits on, to make a fuss of her mum instead of just taking the biscuit tin in with her. There was a brief flashback of a plate with biscuits on, sitting on top of the brochure with a mug of tea. Tea in her favourite mug, a stripy blue and white one that was left in the house by her old aunt. The same mug that she was about to drink out of. The thoughts whirled about in her head while she tried to make sense of them, she recalled some of the tea getting cold while she watched, listening to Mike droning on about the folly and the outbuildings, the land and the pub. Was it the pub he mentioned too? She wasn't sure if she drank anything from the mug, did she? Did she? Sipping her tea from the same mug she tried hard to remember how much she did drink and if it tasted funny or different when she was with Mike. She sighed, realising that she needed to quit thinking about it as she wasn't getting anywhere. She just didn't remember. Shaking her head in frustration, she went to wake her mum up from the sofa.

Her mum wasn't there though, the rumpled blanket was there, but her mum wasn't. She raced back into the kitchen and tried the back door. It was locked. She tried the front door and that was locked too! After looking in every room of the house, Rose was perplexed, her mum wasn't anywhere to be found. She went back to have another look at the sofa to see if she had left her a note or something and looked out of the window. There was a gaggle of people on the other side of the river, pointing at the house. She could see her mum and her dad in the centre of the crowd, with Val and David too. On the periphery was Tom and Steve. Mickey and Bert were some distance away with what looked like Bunty, another Spaniel, and a man that looked like Dennis. There was a lot of arm waving and gesticulating in every direction and her dad seemed to be referring to the brochure. Tom was waving what looked like the paperwork that accompanied the brochure and Steve had another map of some kind, with coloured markings on it.

She immediately saw what was happening. Her family and friends were trying to sort her problems out for her and had started to walk the boundaries of the property using the brochure, maps, and other documentation. Her mum had locked the door behind her, intent on keeping her safe, as mums are prone to do.

She watched as they all walked away up towards the folly and went back into the kitchen to retrieve her cup of tea, she sipped her tea and flicked through the paperwork again, feeling the apprehension and worry rise up again and then flutter back down to her stomach. There was a gnawing feeling in the pit of her stomach again and she reached for a biscuit to settle it. She munched chocolate biscuits and drank tea, her cure all for every ailment, as Mike knew only too well from his behaviour when he was in the house last.

Reading the paperwork again, she was confident that all the inheritance paperwork was watertight, and the land registry documents would stand up to professional scrutiny when she glimpsed a reference to a partnership between a previous occupant of the house and his neighbour. Apparently, they had shared premises for a short while, a very short while, and the document was written to imply that nothing was legally absolved. It was this partnership, this reference that was new to her, totally new.

Thoroughly rattled by this revelation, Rose wanted to be out there with everyone, not shut inside on her own. She wanted to cry, scream, shout, and wail at the world, but first she needed her friends and her parents. Her mum had thought this might happen so her boots were missing from their place by the front door. Her coat was not hanging on the back of the door. With a frustrated cry Rose stomped up the stairs to her bedroom and promptly tripped over the jacket on the floor and her boots that she had last worn at the open day. Both were not suitable for the trek up to the folly, but she was past caring. She put on the boots and flung the jacket on and ran down the stairs. She was astounded when she got to the bottom of the stairs to find that everyone had returned and they were all crammed into her little kitchen, where her mum was filling the kettle and her dad was searching for mugs.

"So, you left me behind, did you? I am so cross with the lot of you! What were you thinking of? What about me, could you all not have waited so we could have gone together? What's the rush?"

Tom answered for everyone, reaching out to her and attempting to grab her hands in his.

"I am sorry you felt that way, we were all so worried when your mum and dad told us about the brochure and what it was all about, that we all wanted to take a look at the land, boundaries, and everything before you woke. We didn't want to distress you any further. You OK?"

Rose snatched her hands away from his and stuffed them in her pocket, with her hands in her pockets she pulled the jacket around her tight. The envelope in her pocket crumpled and rustled, reminding her that it was there. She drew it out and looked at it with a puzzled expression on her face, until she remembered where it had come from and what it was. It was the envelope that she found when Judy was in the house, while she was tending to the mess she had made on the floor and Judy's burnt fingers. Inside the envelope was an old-looking sheet of parchment, folded in three, sealed shut with red wax. It looked important. She held it up to everyone incredulously.

"What have you got there, Rose?" said Tom, coming to her side at the entrance way to the kitchen. "Let me take a photo of that first as it looks old. Better still, someone get their phone running on record just in case."

She made her way to the kitchen work surface in front of the window. Her mum wiped the side down just in case it was wet. She laid a new tea towel out to put the document on and passed Rose a kitchen knife to break the seal. Using the knife carefully, Rose broke the seal and opened the parchment.

## Sixty-Two

The spidery writing was hard to decipher, but odd words could be made out. It was a letter to the Captain from another gentleman, telling him that he no longer wanted to be associated with him and rent and use the Captain's buildings or set foot on the Captain's land from that date forward. The surname was familiar to everyone in the kitchen for it was on the documents and emblazoned on the front of the glossy brochure that everyone had been peering at for so long.

"Well, there you have it, Rose," Steve grinned at Rose and went on, "the official documentation for the house sale and your great aunt's will is spot on, as is the accompanying land registry document. You gave a photocopy of the land registry document to me months ago, when I repaired the wall that runs alongside the footpath and wanted to know if it was in the right place. The only anomaly was the old agreement amongst neighbours that 'our friend' Trevor has brought up. I have no clue how he would even have known about it. It has no legal status and, if you read the small print, he wants to buy the land off you at a reduced price. He was trying to scare you into believing that he was entitled to it in the first place and to smear your good name. Your little set up in the outbuildings is a resounding success, so he wanted people to think that you might sell it so they wouldn't stay and would go elsewhere." Rose's hands shook as she passed the old document to Steve to have a proper look.

Dennis cleared his throat with a stutter and said, "Well I can understand why he is trying to scupper your plans, Rose. I found out that he planned a shared office space on the ground floor of the old pub, well not him, but his nephew, Mike. I was told that his nephew stayed there when it was The Ship back in the summer and thought it would be a good money spinner, if he converted the first floor as apartments and sold them with contained office space as well as a café for refreshments. Looks like you got there first, Rose, with your buildings, he just wanted to scare you off and your new clients to boot!"

There was a stunned silence in the kitchen. Everyone was finding it hard to process everything. Bert and Bunty broke the silence by whining at the back door. Mickey gave Rose a quick farewell hug, "The dogs need some fresh air and so do I, what a lot of nastiness going around. I will be back later on, so save me some cake, won't you?" Dennis followed him out, with Bunty straining against her harness, wanting to catch Bert up. Both men and their dogs walked into the yard and then back along the footpath together.

Then everyone started talking at once. The chatter was purposeful as everyone shared ideas of what Rose should do next. Tea and coffee were made and taken into the back room where every detail was gone over once again. It was now very clear that Trevor was a really nasty piece of work and that the brochure had been carefully worded and the whole charade had been orchestrated by Mike, his nephew, who hadn't gone away for good as everyone had thought.

The mood was more optimistic and because of that Rose kept her thoughts of what happened that afternoon with Mike largely to herself until she felt the need to say, "Mike was over here that afternoon I was unwell, you know. I remember now. He came over to explain the brochure to me, but he picked out all the points he wanted me to worry about, leaving the other stuff out."

Steve looked across at Rose, "Was he in the kitchen at all by himself, Rose?"

Tom cottoned on to what he was getting at immediately, "Oh Rose, was he? Sleeping tablets, surely not? Even he would not do something like that, would he?"

Rose answered truthfully, "I never saw him in the kitchen. He had already let himself in when I got back from meeting with Mr Pernick and Trevor. He had already made me a cup of tea, but I don't remember drinking much or any of it. I don't think I did. I don't know, I really don't. I am so confused."

Rose's dad, Pete, went extremely pale and then very, very red. He was furious that someone had harmed his daughter. Joan put a hand in his to calm him down. "Pete, don't do anything silly. Rose can't remember and you going round to his place and thumping him won't make it any better, but it will make it ten times worse."

Rose shook her head. "I really don't remember. Let's leave it for the time being and deal with Trevor first. Actually, let's not, I am going to deal with Mr Pernick, his solicitor instead. I don't want to give Trevor the time of day."

No one noticed Tom leave the house and wander into the garden by himself.

## *Sixty-Three*

---

Tom slipped out because he wanted to be on his own to deal with his thoughts. He had been working for Trevor and Judy for most of the winter months. He had never seen Trevor but had liked Judy and often chatted to her in his breaks about Rose, her lovely house, and her plans for the future. He had unwittingly given all the details to Trevor through Judy. He had been paid well for his work, but his focus had been in the finer details of the planting and the old roses he had taken off their hands. He was focusing on the old roses when he should have been worrying about 'his' Rose.

Tom had not even made much time for Rose, leaving her alone in the house a lot of the time over the winter months. He was cross with himself for letting her down and letting himself be duped in that way. He liked Judy to talk to, but not in a sexual way. She was always flirting with him, he loved that, but did not find her as attractive as he found Rose.

Rose was the girl for him, but he needed to make it up to her and fast, before Steve took advantage of his stupidity as well.

He looked back at the house and it shimmered in the hazy sunlight. The shrubs moulded together and grew taller in front of his disbelieving eyes. He blinked in amazement as the house had vanished behind the greenery.

The greenery grew brighter and brighter, and the shades of green merged into one vivid emerald green and then the house reappeared in the haze, with several shadows in the doorway. The front door was open, and Rose could be seen standing in the doorway, or was it Rose? Tom couldn't really make out her face. She was standing with shadows all around her.

He walked towards the door and, when he got closer, he saw that it was his Rose, surrounded by shadows that faded as he got closer but reappeared again moments later. Their faces almost clear and recognisable before fading away yet again.

When he was within arm's reach of Rose, he caught a glimpse of the Captain with his arm around her shoulder, holding her tight. The captain met Tom's gaze with his own steely glare and held fast for several moments. Until he was gone once more.

Rose stood at the doorway and reached out to pull Tom in close, knowing how hurt he must be feeling after knowing that it was Trevor all along. He felt a pressure on his arm before he got to Rose and heard a familiar giggle in his ear. He paused for a second till the giggle died away and pulled Rose in tight. They held each other and shared a kiss.

In the hallway, Steve watched them embrace before turning away.

## *Sixty-Four*

Mr Pernick, Trevor's solicitor, was contacted by Rose the following day and she also emailed him a copy of the document that had come to light, making reference to the recent recording that was made when the document was discovered. She firmly stated that she was not interested in selling any land and she would be the first to contest any proposed housing estate to border her land. Mr Pernick had told her that the land surrounding her own was predominantly marsh land, so was extremely unlikely to be suitable for building the vast numbers of houses that his client had proposed in his glossy brochure anyway. It would be very expensive to drain the marshland and the potential for flooding was ever present. Indeed, her house had been very fortunate to escape any flooding the previous year. Mr Pernick promised he would pass the message on to Trevor and to Mike, Trevor's nephew and business partner.

Rose also mentioned that if she saw the pair of them, Trevor or Mike, anywhere near her property she would contemplate filing complaints with the Police, as there were numerous matters that she could make the Police aware of.

"I completely understand where you are coming from, Rose," Mr Pernick agreed. "I won't be doing any more work for them after this. Indeed, after that incident in your yard that day, I told Trevor that it was the final straw and regardless of the massive cheque he was willing to write me, I was no longer prepared to work with him.

Please accept my apologies for everything Trevor has done.

"I shouldn't really tell you, but I will, to put your mind at rest. Trevor was hoping you would just go along with his plans when Mike had managed to sweep you off your feet again. The paperwork probably won't stand up to much scrutiny and the brochure is full of gloss, hot air, and not much substance. It is true that your properties share a boundary but that's about it. I have double checked my paperwork this morning and I am sorry to say that we have both been double crossed. He led me to believe that it was his land. Looking at my copy, that boundary map that he gave you is really inaccurate and designed to shock, scare, and upset you. Totally unacceptable. I am so very sorry, Rose."

After her lengthy conversation with Mr Pernick, Rose felt the urge to walk the boundaries of her property again, so she followed Mowzer as he strolled around the house, seeking the uncomplicated companionship of a cat. She followed him as he trotted along the back of the house and paused when he did to look across at the folly. The crows were once again circling the tower. The folly did not belong to Trevor, however much he wished that that the building was his to make into another modern home for himself and Judy. It was truly part of the Captain's House and would always be so. A pair of magpies flew over her head and settled on the roof of the house. Until one of the magpies flew down and settled at her feet, picking at something silvery in the grass. As she approached, it flew up to join its mate on the roof and she parted the long grass to see what the bird was entranced with. The bell that had fallen off her Christmas tree was still in the grass where it has fallen on Christmas Day. She picked it up and whispered a quiet thank you to the magpie as it flew away again in the direction of the folly. Placing the small silver bell in her pocket to keep it safe, she continued around the house until she was in the front garden.

Mowzer led her to the bottom of the drive and along the hedge towards the big old tree that fell in the non-existent storm. On the way she wondered if it was Mike in the car that was crushed by the tree, or maybe Trevor. Had her captain had anything to do with the tree falling?

As she walked past the huge tree and its exposed roots, her eyes caught a flash, a gleam and little sparkle. She knelt and saw the edge of something glistening in the sun, dug the soil from around it with her hands and teased the object free. She rubbed it with the sleeve of her jumper and the dirt fell away to reveal a locket, inscribed with the words, 'Everything you need is right here'. She wedged her fingernail under the clasp of the locket and prised it open, breaking a nail in her hurry. Another captain's face and his lady looked out at her from the faded photographs within. She sat back on her heels and smiled at her new captain and his lady that looked the image of her old aunt, perhaps this was her aunt's mother, Dorothy, and this captain was her old aunt's father, Albert. Maybe, she mused, maybe …

Then her eye caught the corner of a tin box still buried in the soil, as her hands dug once again in the soil to remove the box, she heard a deep-throated chuckle and an answering giggle in the breeze.

# ABOUT THE AUTHOR

Mel J Wallis lives in Kent and has based her Captain trilogy in the Kent county. She lives in a village on the North Downs with her husband, Andy, and two teenage daughters, Amy and Louise. She shares her home with the family's two cats, Pickle and Kitty, and the garden with their elderly rabbit, Apple.

She enjoys walking the Kent countryside, deep in thought, contemplating her plotlines and developing her characters. In the summer you will find her stretched out in the sunshine in her garden and in the winter curled up in a comfy chair in front of the fire, always with a book in her hands.

She is a passionate volunteer and supporter of several hearing-loss charities, in particular Hearing Link and Hearing Dogs for Deaf People. Living with hearing loss all her life, she is now incredibly lucky to be partnered with her very own Hearing Dog, Lucy.

As a new author, Mel enjoys sharing the adventures of her fictitious captains with her readers in person at events, with book club Q&A's and engaging with her readers as she gets to grips with the joys of social media and virtual chats.